# Across a Field of Starlight

*Across a Field of Starlight* was outlined and thumbnailed in a notebook, then drawn, lettered, and colored digitally using a Wacom tablet and Clip Studio Paint.

 Published in the United States by RH Graphic, an imprint of Random House Children's Books, a division of Penguin Random House LLC, New York.

RH Graphic with the book design is a trademark of Penguin Random House LLC.

Visit us on the web! RHKidsGraphic.com • @RHKidsGraphic

Educators and librarians, for a variety of teaching tools, visit us at RHTeachersLibrarians.com

Library of Congress Cataloging-in-Publication Data is available upon request.
ISBN 978-0-593-12414-7 (hardcover) — ISBN 978-0-593-12413-0 (pbk)
ISBN 978-0-593-12415-4 (ebk)

Designed by Patrick Crotty

MANUFACTURED IN CHINA
10 9 8 7 6 5 4 3 2 1
First Edition

# Across a Field of Starlight

BLUE DELLIQUANTI

## ALSO BY
## BLUE DELLIQUANTI

*Meal* (with Soleil Ho)

*O Human Star*

To those who know a better world is possible.
In solidarity.

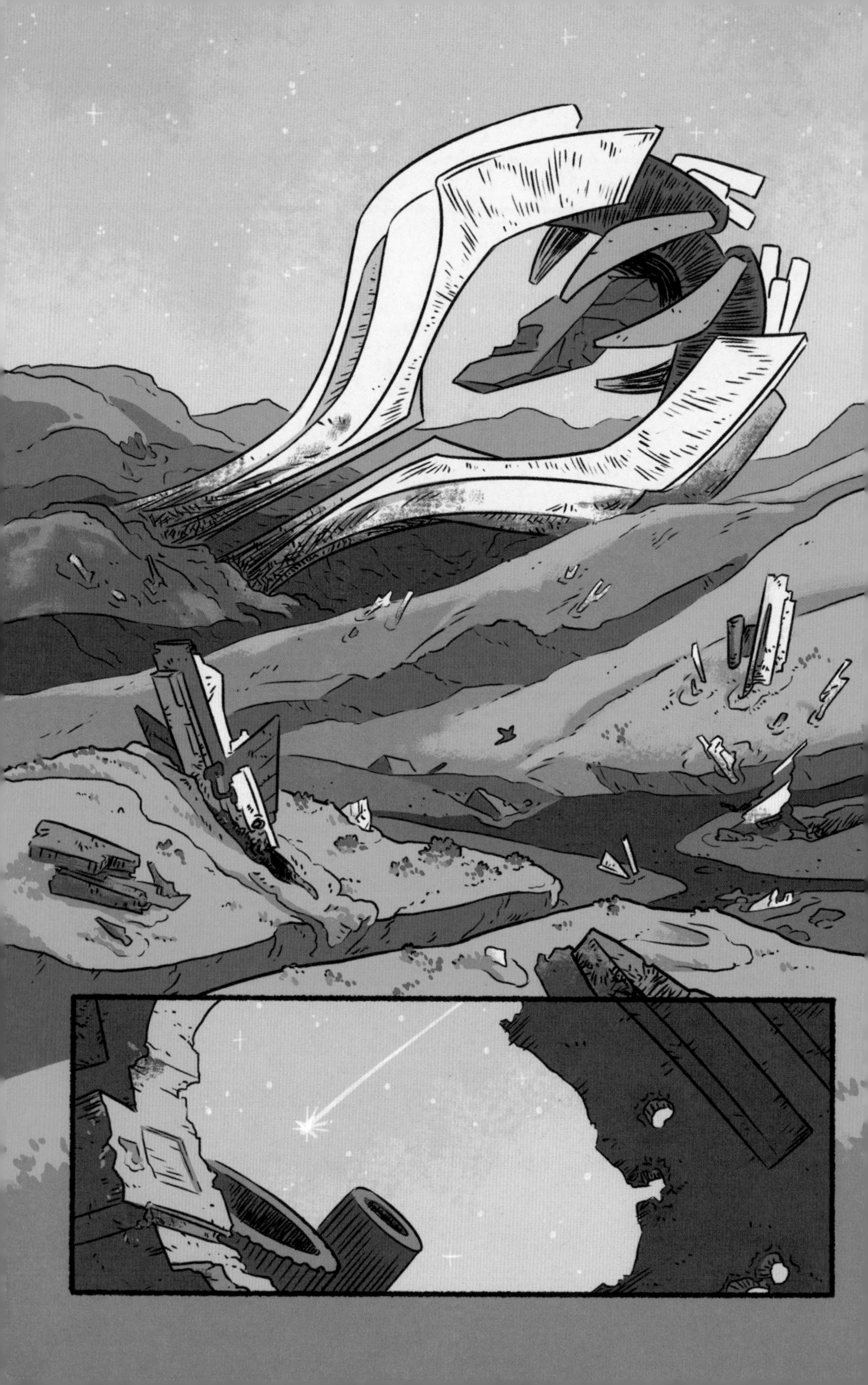

Amazing! Do you see it? Do you see it, Field?
I see it. Have you figured out what kind of ship it is, Lu?

Three layers of shield plating, central boosters . . . it's a Bract class. Gotta be. It's *huge.*
At *least* 600 meters long.
630 for a Bract class.
That would have made it the commanding vessel! A commanding vessel from the Ever-Blossoming Empire and the rebels *still* shot it down!
Is anyone gonna come back for it?
This battle only ended nine days ago. Any survivors would have only just reached the nearest Blossom outpost.
We have some time before they return to pick up their scraps.

Sufficient time to collect biomass from all survey zones.
Thanks, Field.
We've got eight hours of daylight, folks.
Lu, focus in. Are you ready to run your own project?
I set it up already, Pra! It's measuring the particle levels in the atmosphere.
Hey, when I'm done, can I walk out and—
Including the organic compounds?
I already separated the amino acids from the heterocycles and presolar grains. So can I—
And what does that help us learn?

How debris scatters through a planet's lower atmosphere. Now can I *please* look at the ships when I'm done?!

I just want to make sure you're staying on task, kiddo.
Let them go, Pra.

You heard Field. We only have so much time to collect any data at all. Let Lu decide what is and isn't worth learning.
Sigh
I suppose.
Thanks, Auntie!

It's just a shame.
Of course, dear.
So little time to learn from this planet before the war swallows it up again.

We're starting the biomass collection. You coming?
Right, right!
All right, Lu, just check in with Field if you run into any—
—trouble.
Okay.
They're using those drills in the bog, right? For taking chunks out of it?
Only small core samples for the biomass survey. I'm watching Wei analyze the first samples right now. I'm already recording a rich variety of life-forms.
How many?
One moment.
Forty-seven distinct species so far.

And how is *your* project going? What are you—
Who's going through the samples? Wei?
That's right. What kind of readings are you detecting, Lu?
Wei and Pra have had fourteen conversations this whole trip, and only five were research-related. Do they *like* each other?
That is absolutely none of your business.

But you *know*, right? Pra talks to you and so does Wei. They talk to *their* yous, and all of the yous are connected.
Yes, and what they tell me is between them and me.
You wouldn't want me sharing *your* secrets with anyone who asked, would you?

No, I guess not.
Now, between you and me . . .
. . . what have you *really* been following for the last half hour?

An ion trail. The kind left by a spacecraft when it comes through the atmosphere for a landing.
These readings are really hot—it should be up ahead!
Lu—
There it is!
SNAP
Lu, be careful—
A transport shuttle!
SSSSKD

This doesn't look like a Blossom ship. But I can't tell where it's from.
I can't detect any identifying marks or labels. It will be hard to search my limited records for a craft this generic.
SKRRRRT
It's a helmet. Do you think there were any surviv–
Lu!
Huh?!
WHAM

Ngh-

AH!

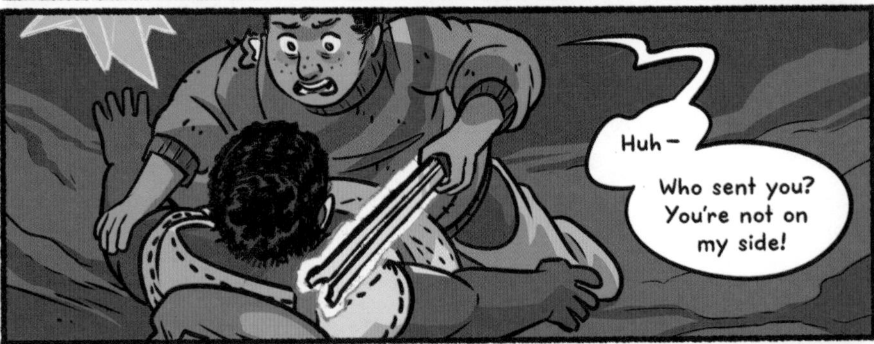
Huh-
Who sent you? You're not on my side!

No tattoo. So you're not from the Empire.
But you have a *robot*-

SSSKR
GH-

SKREEEEEEE
GAH!

SSSKREE
Lu, are you all right?
Uh-huh. They just knocked me down.

I will alert the rest of the research party that a *hostile individual*—
What? No! Field, use common sense!

Nh—
They're just a kid, like me.
And that coat's from a ship's emergency pack.
And there's nobody helping them.

You're all alone.
And you're not Blossom.
No. We won't hurt you again.

GRROWL

You're hungry?
Yeah, um.
D-do you have any food to trade?

Perhaps they should have asked *before* they attacked us with a stunstick.
*Ssh!*

No, listen! We're not enemies, right? You just landed?
So I'll trade you! I took a lot of stuff out of the shuttle.

It's never gonna fly again, so I pulled out, uh, the nav computer, the fuel cells . . .

Anything you could use more of? Is any of this a good trade for a ration pack? I ran out two days ago.

I'm not *begging*, okay? I'm better than that. I have *useful* stuff. I can be useful to you.

Here. I packed some snacks for the trip.
. . . What do you want in exchange?

What? Nothing. It's *food*.

Th-thank you.
It's okay. It's just quickbread.
*Thank you.*

krnch

So I'm gonna look around your shuttle now.

No identification marks on the hull, but . . .
. . . the seats are all different, like they were taken from different ships . . .

. . . and a painting of a bird on the ceiling of the shuttle.
Wow.
It's a fireback.

It's our symbol, you know? For the Fireback Brigade. The biggest resistance force the Ever-Blossoming Empire's ever seen.
Whenever they invade a planet, the Firebacks fight back and help people escape.
Me and my family were part of a convoy, a bunch of ships running away together, on the way to a Fireback base.
We cut through this system because it was supposed to be unpopulated. We were trying to sneak through.
But-but we were surprised by a flotilla of Blossom ships.

A few Fireback ships got away, but a lot more got damaged or - or destroyed.
We crashed on the planet and my— my parents didn't—
...
The shuttle's communication array got messed up.
If any Fireback ships come back through this system, I won't be able to broadcast that I'm still alive.
I can't call for help.

You don't have anyone at all?
Lu. A moment.

Please don't tell me you're thinking about *helping* them.
Why not? There's plenty of room on our ship. We can bring them back with—
*Lu.* Listen to me.

Why did the commune only send a research party to visit this planet *now*?
Because the fighting stopped.
Because the fighters *left*, Lu. We never, *ever* get involved with the war or with anyone on either side. It's too dangerous for us. We can't bring them back.

Still—
Hey, I'm Lu. What was your name?
F - Fassen.

Fassen. We're gonna fix your comms array, okay? We'll make sure you get home.

Well, there is *one* thing we can use to get the shuttle's communications back online.
I found it the third day I was stranded here.
You said you saw that huge Blossom wreck a kilometer away?
The Bract class.
I watched this break off in the atmosphere. This is one of the pieces. See all the antennas? There are signal boosters attached.
They're not too far away. You can't swim over there and remove some boosters to put in your array?
See for yourself. It's more like *slime* than water. And it's deep. See how dark it gets in the middle? What if I fall in and can't get out?

Whoa.
An unusually high viscosity.

I've never seen anything like that on the planet I used to live on. What about you?

THWAK

What did you—
It's a dilatant.
Dilatant?

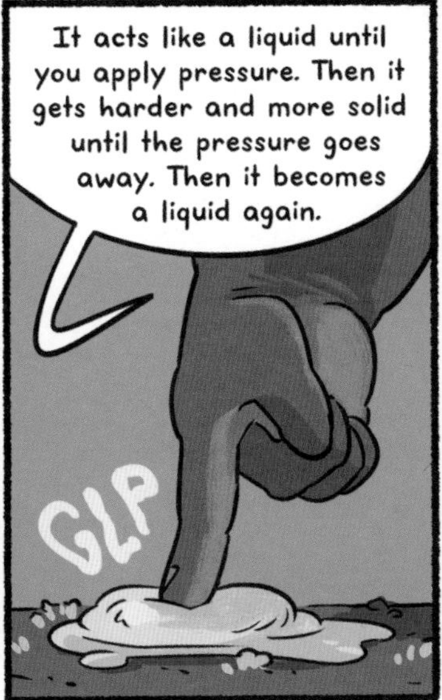
It acts like a liquid until you apply pressure. Then it gets harder and more solid until the pressure goes away. Then it becomes a liquid again.
GLP

I know how we can get you across.

Are –
are you sure?
Pretty sure.
Your weight and
momentum should exert
enough pressure.
As long as you
don't stop running.
Ready?
Yeah.
SLP
It's working!
Lu, it's working!
The rock!
Make sure you
hit the rock!
Now the
flat thing!
Almost there!
Straight ahead!
SL CH

KCHUNK
Can you get it loose?
CHK
Uh-huh! I've almost got it–
SKLOSH
I've got it! I've got it!
Move, Fassen!
No, the rock! Go back and use the rock to pull yourself out!
I'm not going back! I'm almost there!
Grab on!

Gh–
Ha–
Ha ha!

Okay, there we go.
Do the signal boosters fit?

I think so! That ship must have been talking to ships and bases all over the galaxy. I've got enough to tell the Firebacks where I am.

Lu, when they turn that beacon on, I will have to alert the rest of the research party. It's for everyone's safety. And when I alert them, we will have to leave this planet.

For how long?
If the resistance forces return to rescue this child, then this planet may become the site of another battle.

We may *never* be able to come back.
You may never see them again.

Fassen, did you need any more of the signal boosters?
I don't think so. Why?

CHIK
What are you making?
KCHAK
Just a second.

You're calling your people on a special comms channel, right?
Right.
I'm making something the two of us can use to open a channel of our own.
How?

I'm using my device that detects particle radiation.
Now it'll convert its readings into an access code, and that code'll open a channel to any other point in space that has the same particle readings.

We could be thousands of light-years apart—
—but if we're both standing in places with the same kind of background radiation—

—these devices will tune into the same channel—
—and we can talk to each other.
KCHAK
And since we don't have to be anywhere near each other . . .
. . . and I won't end up near any battles or fighting or Empire—
—you don't need to tell anyone else in the commune about this. It'll be a *secret.* Between you and me.
I don't like where this is going.
. . . as long as you're not putting anyone in the commune in any danger . . .
Great! Then it's settled.
Lu, I-I don't understand why you're doing all this for me. If you're not on my side—
No one should ever be alone the way you were.
Let's stay friends, okay?
BWEEP

Incoming message from the ship, Lu.
Kiddo, Field just detected a distress call from the planet's surface. We have to leave before anyone arrives. Fun's over.
On my way, Pra!
You can keep the rest of the snacks, Fassen. I–
Goodbye, Lu.
Talk to you soon.

There you are! Get on board, we gotta move!

We are clear for takeoff.

Incoming orders, squadron.
We're investigating a distress beacon at the source of the skirmish on Yukul-C nine days ago.

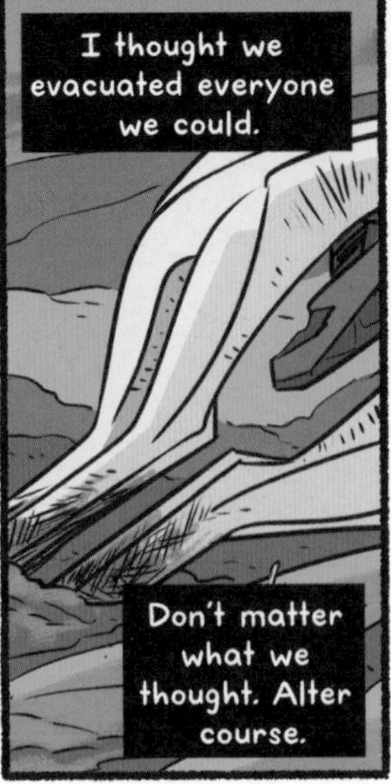
I thought we evacuated everyone we could.
Don't matter what we thought. Alter course.

Altering course now.

# Across a Field of Starlight

Blue Delliquanti

Krik
krak
MWEHHH

tsk

SEARCHING FOR PRESET CHANNEL...

C'mon, c'mon. Lemme get in range.
Krak
Krik
Krak

Fassen! There you are!

We've got less than an hour before the operation!
What're you doing up here?
Oh! Kerro! You caught me, I was just, uh . . .
. . . scanning the horizon for the target.
Fassen, we've talked about this. *It's not your job.*
And if we're not at the site by the time of the operation we're no good to *anyone*. C'mon.
I'll take that one.
You're kidding. You got *another* full set?
Three, four, and five of waters. Green's my lucky color today.

And nobody's dealing any stars. Nheyu, are you hoarding them?

Should've stuck with stones. You owe him five rations now.
Hey, look who got dragged back to camp!

How was your *scouting mission,* Fassen? Any good intel?
Lay off 'em, Peller.

Aw, c'mon, Kerro, it's cute when they play soldier.
Not content with being a junior-grade medic cadet, Fassen? Not enough glory for you?

Of course not, Peller, haven't you heard Fassen's story? Kid got picked up from a deserted planet after getting marooned there in a skirmish.
Fancy! No wonder Sergeant Bda thinks they're *worth* something!
Thirty minutes. Check your tool kit.
Special treatment for the snot-nosed kid who can't set a bone or hit a target!
*Fassen.* Check your armor.
T-minus thirty, troops!
Get to your positions.
*Yes, Sarge!*
Visibility?
Drop ship passing overhead now, Sarge.

VVVV

VVVVVV

VVOOOO
It's *enormous.*
Yeah, but this is the lowest it can fly. Size does you no favors on Tsanggho.
Listen up, squad. Home base predicts it's going to make five drops.

The Blossom learned their lesson after conditions on the surface wore down their original base. They're setting the new base right above their new mine.
DROPOFF
AMBUSH
DESTINATION
Their cruisers are too big to land here, so they're dropping down supply convoys in the Gr, Ibben, and Mne Valleys. All convoys will be targeted on the most difficult terrain of each route.
No empire invades the Gr Valley and gets away with it.
You ready? I can't do my job if you aren't focused.
Ready.
Sucks that we got stuck with the convoy carrying medical supplies. What about the one with the tools? The weapons?
You just wish you were in *his* squad.
Are you kidding me? I'd pirate the convoy with the *bathroom* supplies if it meant I got to be in *Nide's* squad!

You know how many bots he took out in his last sortie? Twenty-three.
Single-handed. What a legend.
Squad!
We have visuals.
Blackout?
Ready and waiting for target to enter range.

FWEE

Team Two, hold your position. Team One, with me.
KRKLKLKLKL
What the-
KRAK

PCHAK
It's an ambush! Report to command–
Comms are down! They blacked out our comms!

KRAK
That's three for me!
Four!
THWIP

Path clear! Time to inspect!

Any casualties?
None. Cargo's all yours.

Check the crates and seals. Make sure nothing looks like it was tampered with.

Anesthetics, anticonvulsives – *vitamins!* I haven't seen a vitamin in *weeks.*

Any broken seals, Fassen?

The wall! Move!
What-?
KRAK
KRAK
GAH!
They're hanging from the cliff wall!
Fassen, get away from there!

PCHAK
How many?
Four!
KRAK
Covering fire! Up front!
PCHAK
KRAK
One down on the right side!

Medic!
On my way!
Fassen! Hand out triage tags.
On it!
Minor tag? My arm got blasted!
You're not losing too much blood. You can walk, so you can wait.
Besides, green's your lucky color.
Two left! Team Two, push them away from the perimeter!
They're turning around!

Aim high!
Force them to hang low to the ground!
That one's not firing!
Is it trying to run?
It's trying to escape the blackout zone.
It's going to call for help! Don't let it fly past!
Cadet, get *down*—

KTHUNK
The hell?

Get off!
Nh-
Gah!

SPLOSH
C'mon, c'mon! How do I—
KRAK
Ah!
KRAK
KRAK

krk|k|k|k|
krsh
sKREEEE
ENEMY COMBATANT ON GLIDER FIVE POINT FOUR, REPEAT–
KRAK
BLACKOUTS STILL IN EFFECT ON ROUTES ONE, TWO, AND FIVE. TARGET IS–

-ON THE MOVE, ALL SQUADRONS-
-VISUALS CONFIRMED-
-CAN'T GET A LOCK ON HIM-
-TOO FAST-
KRAK
-GLIDER FIVE POINT THREE IS DOWN, REPEAT-
KROOM
-GLIDER DOWN-
-ALL SQUADS-

What does that mean? Hang back?
Flat? Press flat?
How'd the pilot do that clingy thing?
VRRRRRM
VRP
VRP
VRP
KSPLOSH

POHAK
KRAK
VRRRRRRRRRRR
THWAK
Whoa! Did I look that cool when I did it?

Okay, careful—

The summit!

The channel!

SEARCHING...
CHANNEL DETECTED
DOWNLOAD MESSAGE?
[Y / N]

Yes!
Yes - yes - yes!
MESSAGE DOWNLOADED
VIEW NOW? [ Y / N ]
The convoy!
You're killing me, Fassen.
You can't keep pulling stunts like this!

I did more good this time than any time I've tried doing medic stuff.
That's not the point, Fassen! You can't just abandon your post!
The sergeant is gonna eat you *alive* for this. You'll be lucky if she *ever* lets you go out on another sortie.

Greetings to you, elder.
Welcome back, Sertig. More toys to keep in your toy chest?
I was always taught to keep my room clean.

KRNKRN

RRRN

KRNKRNKRNKRNKR

THE FIRST TO RESIST
THE LAST TO FALL

Cadet Fassen Ruust!

I will not stand for dereliction of duty in my squad, cadet. You were there to tally supplies and provide medical aid. Not to *joyride.*
Y-yes, Sarge.

You've been assigned to fulfill your training in the medical track, not the combat track. But if this happens again you will find yourself on *neither.*

You're kidding me. That was a cadet on that glider?

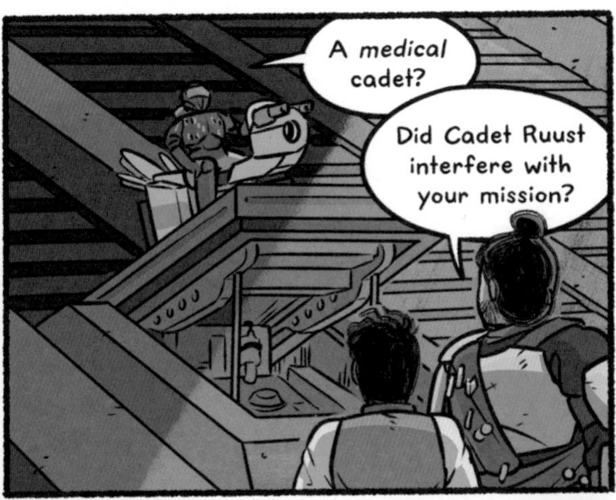
A *medical* cadet?
Did Cadet Ruust interfere with your mission?

Interfere? Nah.

There wasn't anything I couldn't handle.

*Nide Lumen!*

Those gliders are brand-new Blossom tech. How'd you manage to fly one so easily?
I-I'm not sure. I was barely able to spot them hanging from the cliff.
Cadet Ruust did alert the squad to the gliders' presence.

Have you ever flown *anything* before?
No. I just . . . used my instincts?

How come you've been hiding a *pilot* from me?
I'm directing the cadet's considerable talents toward improved performance of their *assigned* duties.
Ohhhh, you're *disciplining* them. May I suggest that you commute their punishment somewhat?
Given the circumstances . . .

Cadet Ruust! Your punishment will be capped at ten cleaning shifts in the medical wing.
Yes, Sarge!

An excellent idea, Sergeant Bda. Join me for a debriefing session?

Very well, Captain.

SQUEAK
SQUEAK

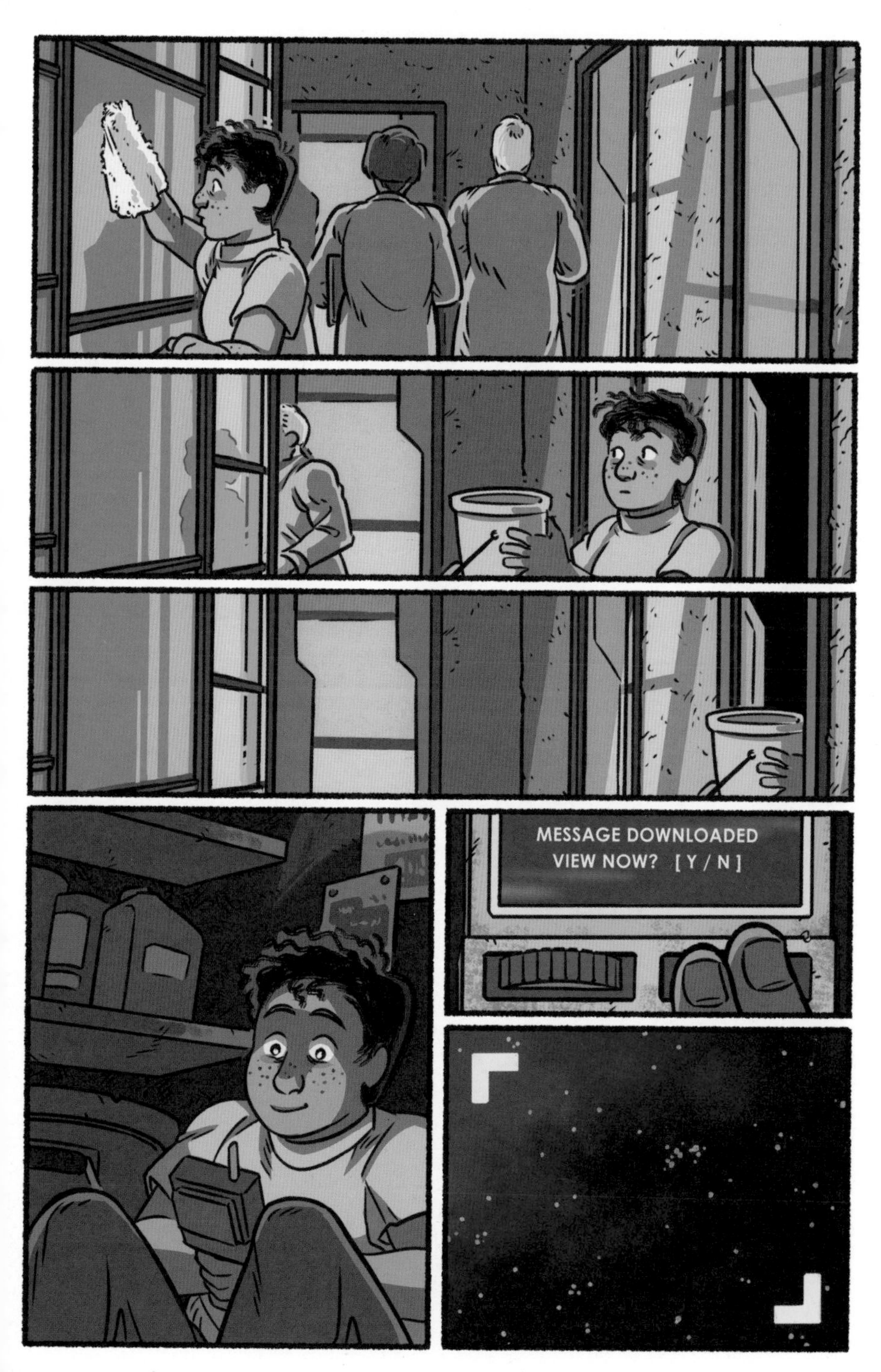
MESSAGE DOWNLOADED
VIEW NOW? [ Y / N ]

Found a new place to access the channel. Pretty, huh?
Oh, it's budding! I wondered when it would.
Hold on, hold on, let me show you–
–the progress I made on the model. I'm adding the engines right now, I sanded the inside, and–
–I made some crew members! Say hello to Captain Sparks and Commander Mehr!
I tried to match your drawings the best I could. What do you think?

The faces were painted with a high degree of accuracy.
Thanks, Field!
Field, say hi.
Hello.
The model's turning out so good, Fassen.
I wish you were here working on it with me, though.
My aunt saved me a lot of scrap from her last project, and I've been digging through it to see if there's anything good we can add to the starship Quickbread.

Oh, and I've been drawing the new robot character! Here's a new outfit I designed for when it joins the crew.
Speaking of which–
I have some questions I wanted to ask you after your last message. About the new story.
I know you said Captain Sparks would be suspicious of the new crewman after the *Quickbread* escaped from the hostile robots on the mining asteroid, but listen to this.
What if Doctor Drupe is the one who decides to give the robot a chance? Maybe she asks it to help in the sick bay and–

—and she realizes this robot isn't like the others in the mines.
Oh, come on, Lu.
Maybe she teaches it to dress wounds and play the flute and—
Like *that'll* do any good when the other robots attack the ship!
—and then it— it helps out during the next space battle! Maybe it even saves Commander Mehr from an explosion or something!
Okay, now we're talking.
So Captain Sparks sees that and says—
As a world resisting colonization by the Ever-Blossoming Empire . . .

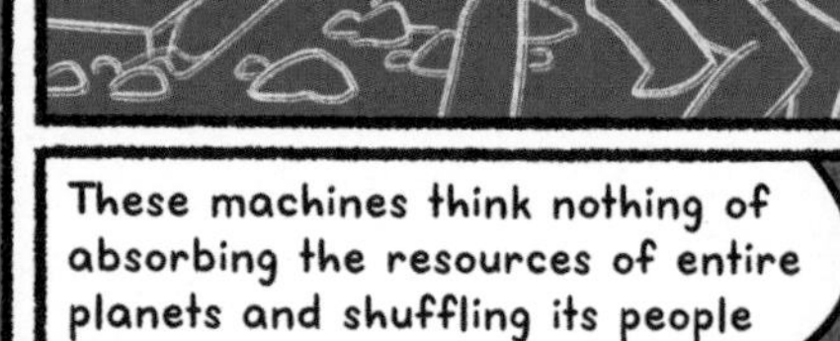

However, the cult of personality that comes with a human figurehead encourages blind obedience among the Empire's citizens. Can anyone tell me—

LOCKDOWN IN EFFECT!

Another volley. Who's barricading today?
I will.
Your classmate Sha has elected to help protect the room against the Empire's attack. Thank him for his service.
SHELTER

KRNKRNKR

Thank you for your service, Sha.

Man, and it was almost lunchtime, too.
Betcha this one only lasts an hour.
Don't get my hopes up.

Fassen! Bring me some potassium iodide and blueprint powder!

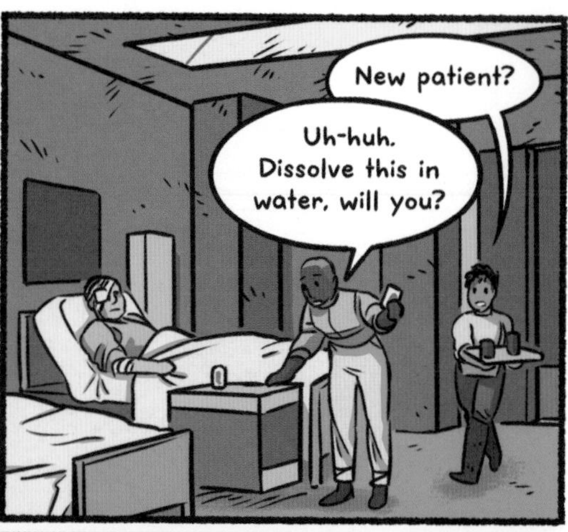
New patient?
Uh-huh. Dissolve this in water, will you?

How long before you realized there was a crack in the shield?
I dunno, five minutes?

Sounds like it's only a mild case of radiation poisoning. The headache should go away.
Good. I gotta pick up another shift to pay this off.

What shield are they talking about?
The one protecting the communications array. You know how that works?
Uh—

So you know how the Fireback ships all around the planet receive their orders instantly? Like, the second we send 'em? That's 'cause we're all surrounded by the same mix of special particles. And those particles resonate with each other no matter how far apart they are. Each specific concentration of particles is called a *channel.*

You find all kinds of channels pressed next to each other, like layers of rock in a mountain. And sometimes, on the other side of the galaxy, you can detect those special particles in the same concentrations you'd find in the ones back home. Anyone standing within that concentration of particles can access *your* channel, too.

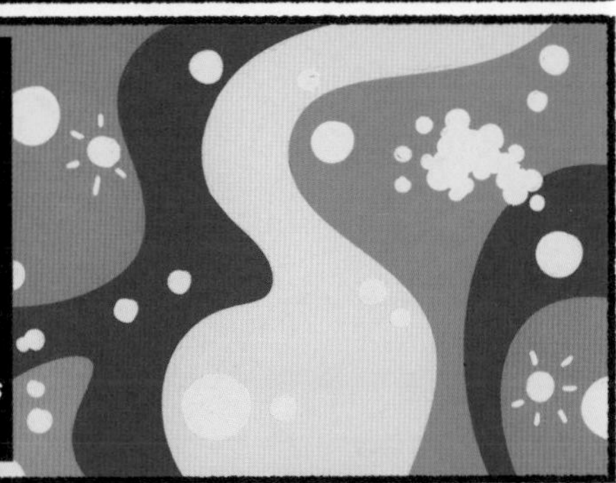

So you can talk to someone on a faraway planet as long as you can both access the same channel. Even if it'd take you years in the fastest ship to reach that planet yourself!

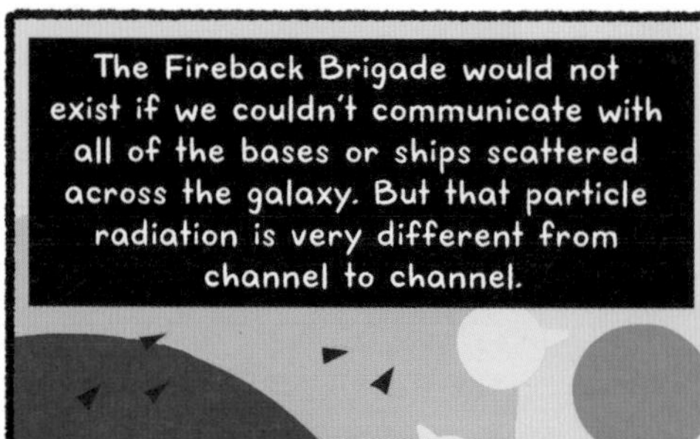
The Fireback Brigade would not exist if we couldn't communicate with all of the bases or ships scattered across the galaxy. But that particle radiation is very different from channel to channel.

Tell me, Fassen, how do you solve this problem?
You'd have to change the radiation, right? Change the—the mix of particles your communicator detects?

Precisely. We use a machine called an *anchor* to change the base's channel.
We can speak to a ship on one side of the galaxy, change the channel, and then speak to a base on an asteroid thousands of light-years in the other direction.

However, the energy the anchor gives off can make its technicians extremely sick. So we *shield* the anchor with a certain kind of metal.

The Ever-Blossoming Empire carries anchors aboard its largest warships. Intel believes that their operators are something *other* than illness-prone humans.

Don't go telling robot stories, Doc. You'll have Fassen quaking in their boots.
I'm—I'm not scared of *robots*!
Uh-huh.
I'll fight a robot any day of the week!
Good morning, Sergeant.
S—Sarge?
Doctor. I'm here to escort Cadet Ruust.

Follow me.

WHAT SACRIFICE HAVE *YOU* MADE FOR FREEDOM TODAY?

Is this all . . .

. . . stuff from the ambushed convoys?

I have retrieved Cadet Ruust.
Oh, awesome! Thanks, Sertig.

How's cleaning duty treating you, Fassen?

Sertig told me the whole story. Saving her from enemy fire, drawing away an enemy attack . . .

Color me impressed!
Captain Helvedine Lumen.

Call me Nide.
I—I saw you take on all those Blossom drones. When you took that soldier's speeder—

Oh yeah, my new ride! We got a lot of interesting souvenirs out of that ambush mission. We're storing them all here in the depot.
They were going to the new mining colony, right?

We think the Empire might have bigger plans for our little rock. See all these tools and weapons? You don't need that much muscle if you're just digging up metals.

But *these* crates were under the highest security detail I've ever fought my way through.

Wanna see what's inside?
KLIK

What–

What *is* it?

Well, Fassen, that's what we're starting to figure out.

It looks like a suit of some kind. Can you wear this?
It's got sleeves. Slip one over your dominant arm.

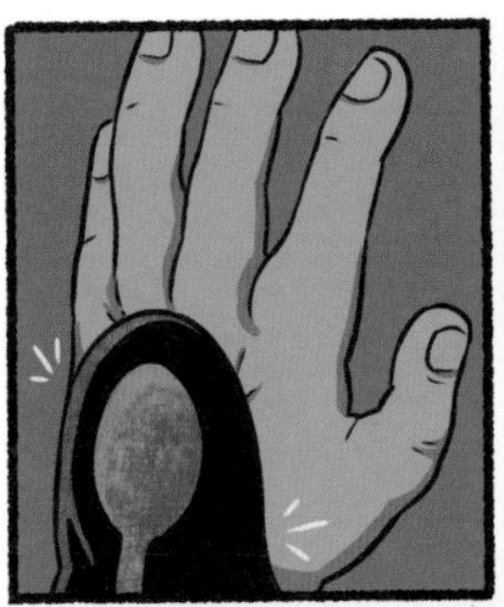

It's shrinking around my arm.
Hold it out.

O-okay?
Just hang tight. We rigged up a device to test its basic functions.

Don't freak out, kid.

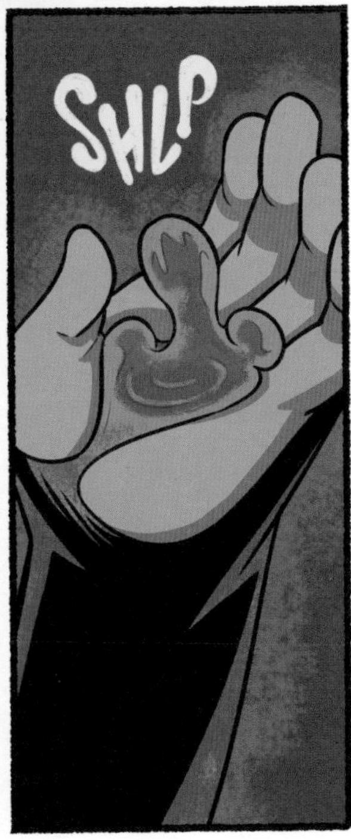
SHLP

SHLLLP
nh-
It's in my mouth! Get it off! I can't -
Take deep breaths! You'll get used to it.
hh
hh
hh
Wh-what is this-
You're doing great, kid. Look up. Recognize anything?
Th-the hovercraft.
Right. We deactivated the engine.

Try getting it off the ground again.
You mean, lift it?
Give it a try.
hup
kreeek
KRAASH

AHAHAHA! Ha!
That hovercraft was still in fine condition.
All right, test over.

I don't understand. Did the suit give me the strength to do that?

That's only a *fraction* of what the suits can do.
This is the most advanced Blossom tech we've ever pilfered, and they're mad as hell that we have it.

We think these suits were designed to function in the vacuum of space, but who knows what *else* they're capable of?

The Brigade leadership have given the captain the authority to learn as much about the suits as possible and assemble a squadron to put them to good use.
Anything to protect Tsanggho against those encroaching *weeds*.

What's it like to have that power at your fingertips, Fassen?
We could use your enthusiasm behind that power. And your skills.
What do you say, kid? Want to join me?

Okay, *maybe* Doctor Drupe can teach the robot about, y'know, medical stuff. It'd come in really handy if we decided to throw the crew into another space battle.

Maybe it could even save someone with its super strength, you know? That would be cool. Lemme write that down.

But why would she waste time teaching it about her favorite instruments? Even if it learned how to copy the motions, robots wouldn't understand what music is.

It's a *tool.* Like a rifle or a beam glove. It can't be *friends.*

Besides, I always shipped Doctor Drupe with Commander Mehr anyway.

Hey, Field?
Yes?

Do me a favor? Read the particle levels outside and memorize them, please.

I gotta plot them to my map after this is done.
All right.

Look, I even drew its little outfit. Maybe we could–

BEEP BEEP

incoming message from
CORE STATION
BEEP

Oh, shoot—
One sec—
Hello, Lu. How are you, dear?
Oh! Hi, Auntie. You working at the core today?
Just helping out with a few odd tasks, you know how I like to do.
Field let me know your ship was reaching the border so I thought I'd give you the advisory message myself.
Will you be all right with just your mobile Field? How long will you be out?

Just for the day.
I'm taking particle readings while we sweep the border.

You're a good kid. Always helping out.
Just run back and holler if you run into soldiers or anything at all.

Don't be a hero. Stay safe.
BWEEP

Phew.

Shall I resume your secret communiqué from the soldier?
Hey!

When'd you get so *snarky?*

Read me those numbers again?
—and that's when the *Quickbread* receives an incoming message from the mining asteroid—

Frequency: 857.
Photon redshift: 11.1.
Baryon density: -1.2.
So that means I'm using . . . this color! Cool!

We just discovered a new channel right on the edge of Field space. Not one I can reach Fassen at, though. I'd have to take us back to the Dalab system for that.
You've done a lot of work to stay in touch with that child.

And incidentally, this is the last call for fresh food.
Oh, right! Fruit, please.

Of *course* I've done the work. Fassen's my *friend.* And now I know where in the galaxy I have to go to talk to them.

You can skip through this part. I didn't finish the bit where they started talking about the suits.

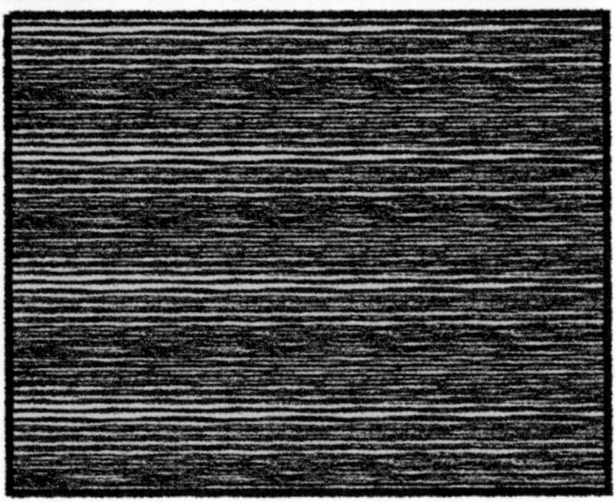

Okay, I'm back. Captain Lumen's started training us while we're waiting for the suits.

He's so cool. He's told us stories about some of the missions he's run, boarding Empire vessels.

Sounds like a typical Fireback showoff to me.
Ssh! Suits.

That's what the suits are, something he stole off a Blossom ship. They're really strange – you wear one, and there's like this goo that comes out of the seams on the suit?

And it flowed around my arms and covered my head, which was scary. But I could still see through it.
And breathe, too. Even though at first it felt like when I swallow water the wrong way.

I wanna try it again. But Captain Lumen's putting us through more training. It's lots of exercise, but it's way more fun than the training I was getting as a medic.

But here's the most exciting part about being in an elite squadron–
The suit! More about the suit!

We eat in a different mess hall! And the food's way better!
Ugh!

I snuck out some extras. Look at this, Lu!
Meat floss buns! I haven't seen these since I was little!
krnch
And I can just *take* them! As many as I want! It all gets charged to my new account.
Field . . .
. . . do you think it was a mistake not to bring them back with us? When we had the chance?

Lu, we've talked about this. We do border sweeps in the first place to make sure the war doesn't reach us. War's brought in by soldiers. And Fassen's a *soldier* now.

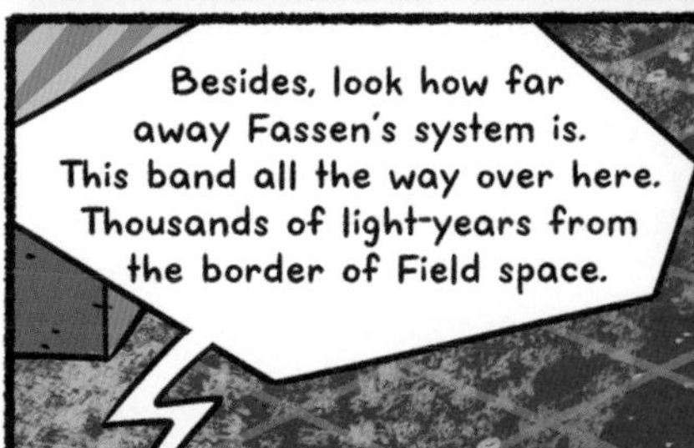


If you wanted to fly all the way out there . . .

tip tip tip
I know. It's just . . .

It's not fair.
No. It isn't.
tip tap tip tap

BAM

What was that?
This area is saturated with much larger pieces of debris. I'll scan ahead as far as I'm able.

Okay. Guess I'll do some steering. Gimme a—
Down starboard. Now.

GAH!
What in the world-

Is that . . . a ship?
I have no record of a ship that looks anything like this.

Mind the debris.
Wait, look at that! That's a life-support system!

Like the one Auntie and I salvaged from a Blossom derelict.
But why is it on the *outside?*

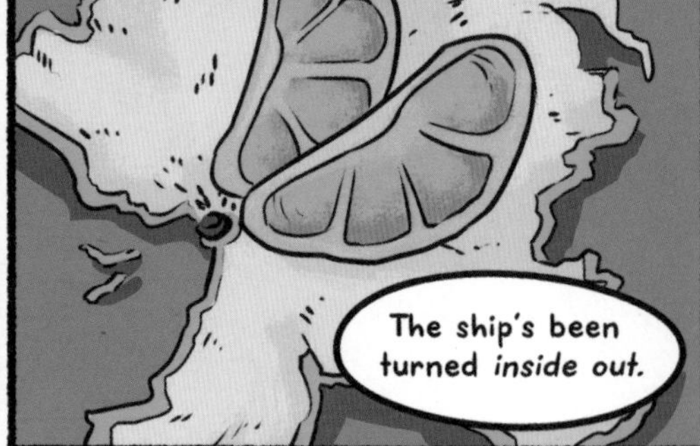
The ship's been turned *inside out.*

Highly improbable.
The amount of energy it would take to tear apart a ship of this size and calculated volume would be –
Field.
There's a life-support system. Where are the people?

A very good question.
I see none, dead or alive.

Let's try finding the cockpit.

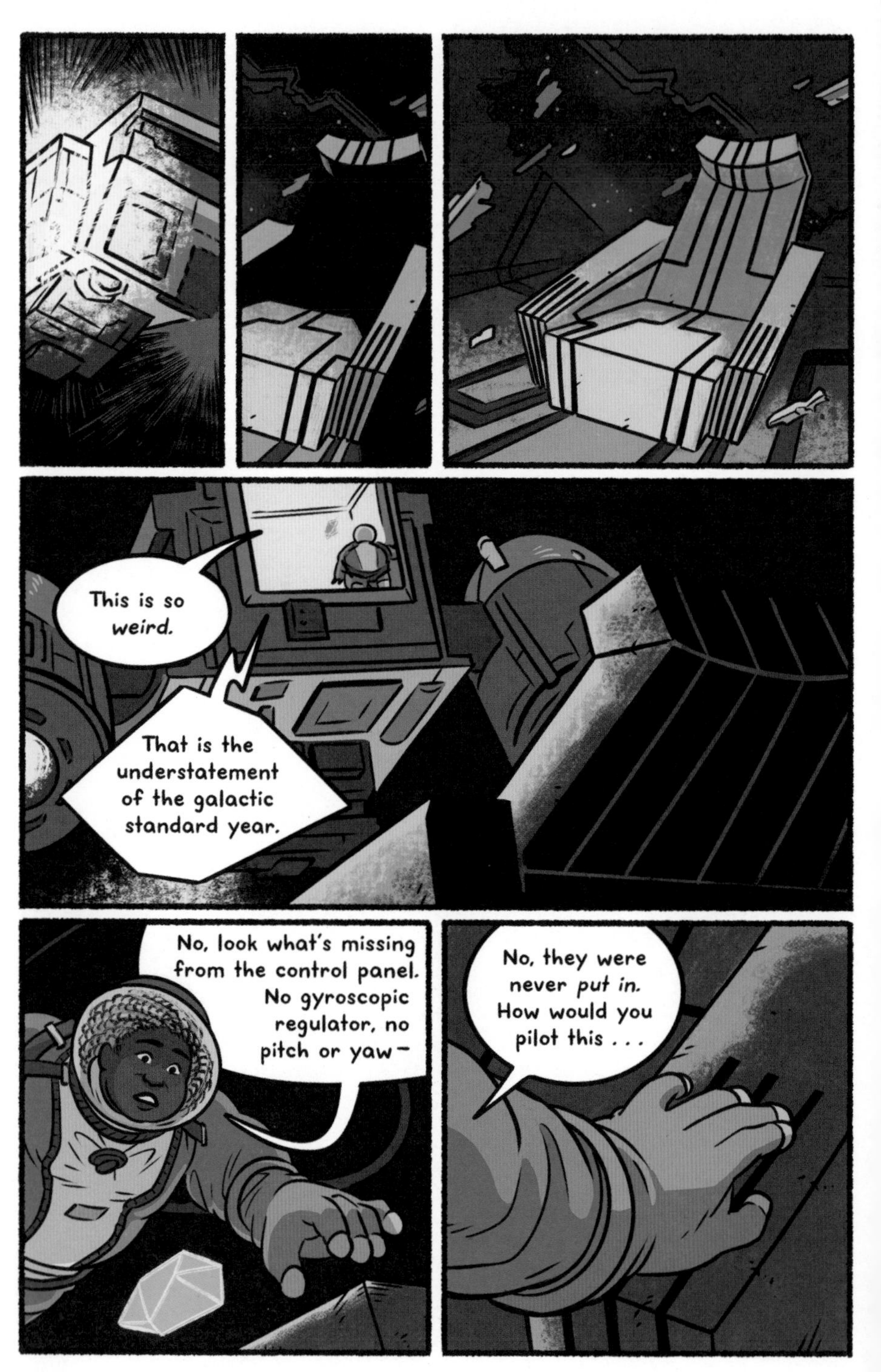
This is so *weird.*
That is the understatement of the galactic standard year.
No, look what's missing from the control panel. No gyroscopic regulator, no pitch or yaw—
No, they were never *put in.* How would you pilot this . . .

Yech!

Whoa.

A liquid in outer space. Very few substances remain in their liquid state when it's this cold. This is—
So weird.

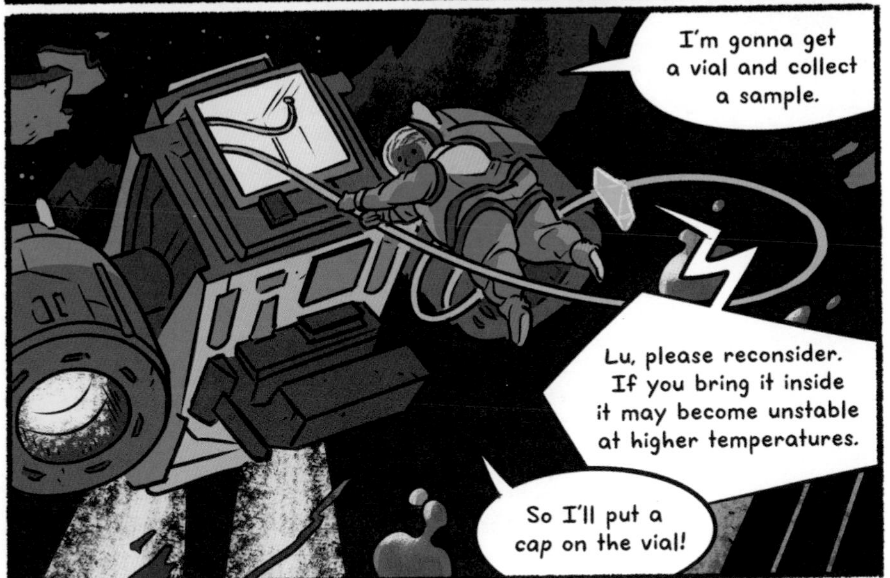
I'm gonna get a vial and collect a sample.
Lu, please reconsider. If you bring it inside it may become unstable at higher temperatures.
So I'll put a cap on the vial!

Lu. This is precisely the sort of discovery we are encouraged to report to the commune once we get back in range.
Out here I can't access my banks of information to tell you what kind of Blossom ship this is. We should go back and—
Field, don't you get it?
That stuff is like the stuff Fassen described! Same color, same texture, same origin.
If I can study it, I can help Fassen. But that means I can't have folks at home asking too many questions.
But the *ship*—
I'll report the ship when we get back. I promise. Just lemme study the goo on my own for now, okay?
It's just a *half* secret.

I dislike this growing collection of half secrets.

T-ten laps complete, Captain.
Don't stop now!

Obstacle course! Let's go, let's go, let's *go*!

Those officers behind Nide . . .

C - Cadet Fassen Ruust. It's an honor to be part of the—
At ease.
Captain Lumen, you said there were eight total. Where is the eighth member of your squad?

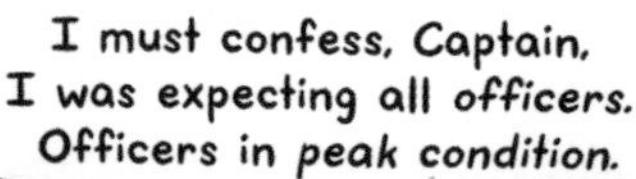
I must confess, Captain, I was expecting all *officers.* Officers in *peak condition.*

Just you wait.
Sergeant Bda! Show us what you can do.

Very well.

FMP
SHF
SSSKD

You see, General, I've recruited not just for aptitude—

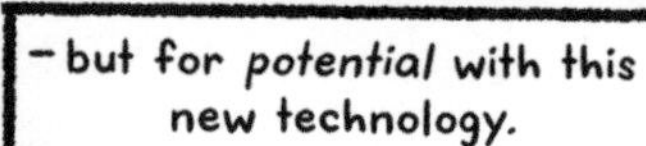
—but for *potential* with this new technology.

In the end it doesn't matter how well we can sharpen these soldiers to fit into the scabbard at our belt—

SNAP

THMP
–because with the suits we become a different kind of weapon *entirely.*

MWEHHH
MEH
MWE

MEHHHKR
Young guest!
We have a Blossom ship incoming! Help me seal the gate!
MEHR
What? But – Intel didn't warn about a ship! They wouldn't have let me go up!
MEHR
The *flock* knows, even when you don't! I'll take the wheel, you run the switch!
MEHR
MEH
KRNKRNKRN
RRRMBL
MEHH

VVOOOOOOOOO
It's moved on. You can go.
Will the animals be okay?
They're used to it.
Thanks for the tip about the early warning system.
What was your name?
. . . Ten Gr Daari.
Cadet Fassen Ruust.

You there?
Uh-huh. Can you see me?
Crystal clear.

It's great being able to actually *talk* to you instead of just sending messages back and forth.

I know. You *never* used to be able to talk at the same time I was in range, though. How are you managing it now?

The squad, Lu! I've got a *passkey* now. I'm allowed to go up into the village in between enemy raids.
Getting my butt kicked in training is totally worth all this *freedom!*

Oh, uh.
What have they been making you do? In training?
Martial arts. Combat. Stuff that teaches us better physical control so we don't, y'know, do anything in the suits we don't *mean* to do.
Have you gotten to wear the suit again, then?

Not yet. But I've been paying attention to Nide wearing it, like you asked. And he's definitely not controlling the armor with a remote this time.
He just thinks and the suit responds.
You mean, it picks up the brain's electrical impulses and acts on them?
That's what I was hoping for! Here, lemme show you something.
I have a goo update!
Field analyzed its molecular structure and hypothesized that it can carry an electrical charge. So I designed this setup to test it.

Okay, so the sample flows from the vial to this metal dish. It doesn't react to any of the things I gave it to play with.

Now I'm gonna borrow Captain Sparks—
Why does he have a battery strapped to him?
You'll see.

All right . . .
Thank you for your service, Captain.
Then I'm gonna set him on the plate, too.
The goo's not doing anything.

Not yet. I'm gonna activate the circuit on the battery. Watch this.
KLIK

GLP

Look. As soon as it sensed an electrical charge, it reacted.

And it did the exact same thing as the suits.

So this is definitely the same stuff the suits are made of, right?
It's very, very likely. The question is what they were using it for on the Blossom ship.

It *might* just be a new kind of space suit. It'd be easier to turn this on and move around in than the bulky suit *I* wear.
But, Fassen, if this is how it behaves when it has an energy source . . .
. . . who knows what else it can do?

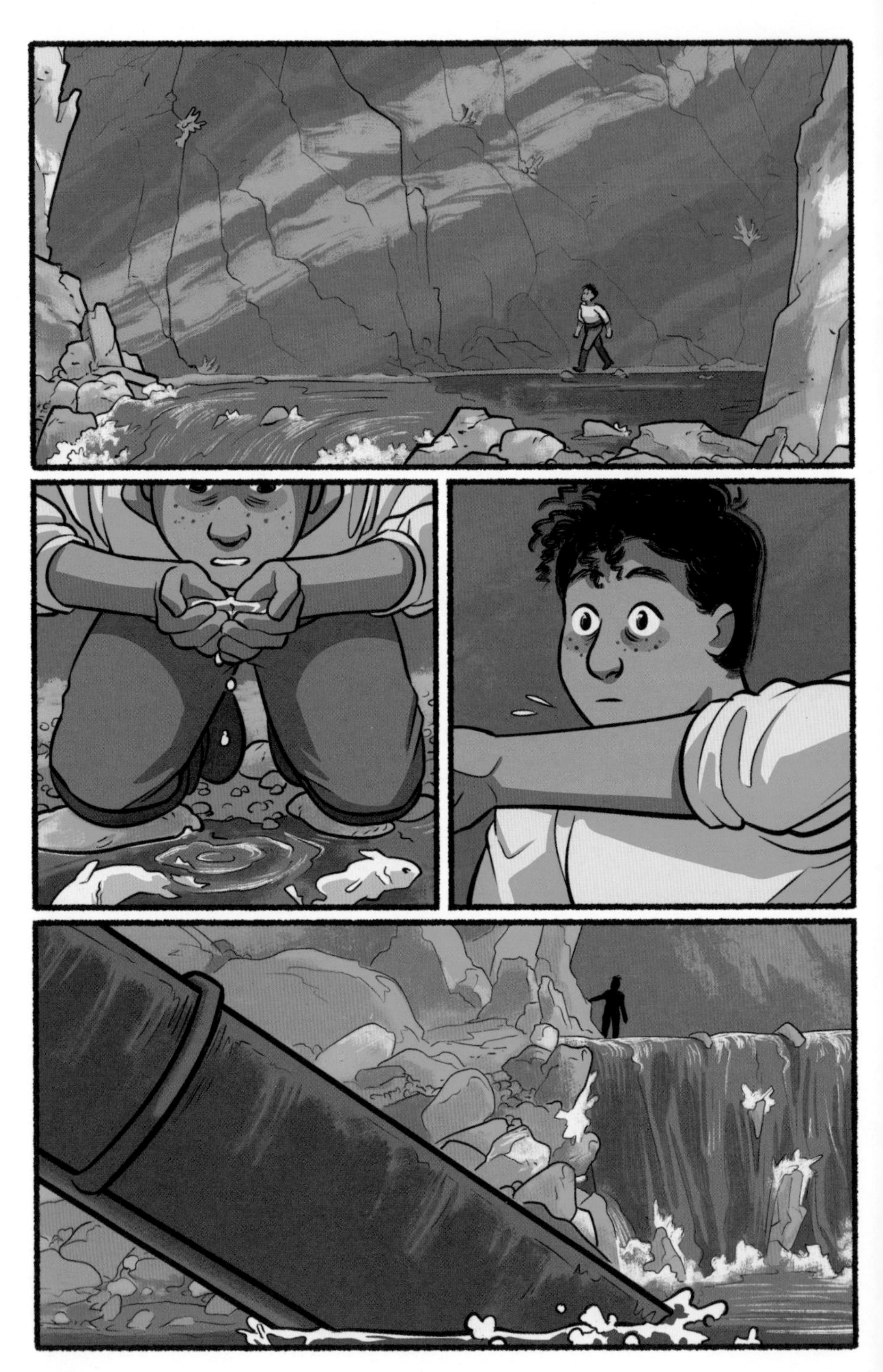

They're mining . . . using water?
KRAKOOM

Those guys . . .
. . . are from the valleys!

PCHAK

PCHAK
KRAK

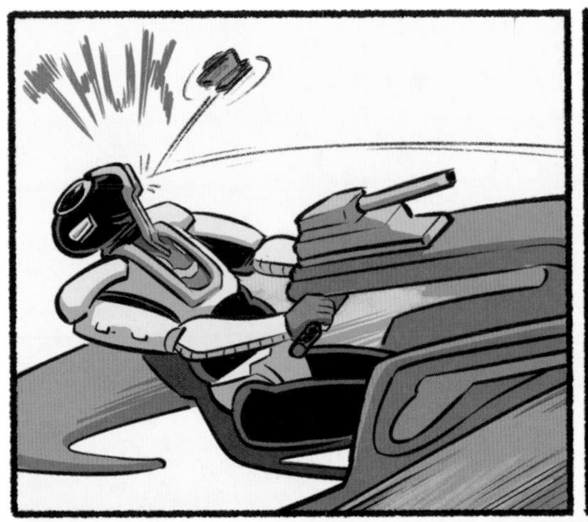
THUK

Are you okay?

A *guest.*
Is there a Fireback strike incoming?

Uh-

KRAK

PCHAK
PCHAK

No!

KRAK
KRAK

RRRMBL

krik
krak

PCHAK
PCHAK
koff koff

I guess the Blossom base can't use this water now.
No one can.

Just another sacrifice to help our guests defeat the Empire.
SSSH!

Next!
BLRRF
Avet! This is the one you're *not* supposed to throw up after!
Tell that to my *stomach*, Hilma!
Ruust! You're up!
Don't close your eyes.
Don't close your eyes.

Don't . . .
. . . close . . .
. . . your eyes.

Two . . .
three . . .

Fourteen . . .
. . . fifteen!

Chalk Fassen up on the no-barf board!
How'd you do it, small fry?
Well, I, um—

I-I've been in a shuttle flight worse than that.
Lemme go get some water.

INSERT PAYMENT TO ACTIVATE
BEEP

. . . prepared for this, Captain?
Absolutely. We've tested the suits and we can get the squad fitted in them by next week.

Yes, about the squad. Zhalanayat and I are concerned about the *liability* that might come with some of your choices.
Like the officer cadet. Or Sergeant Bda. I know you two are *close*—

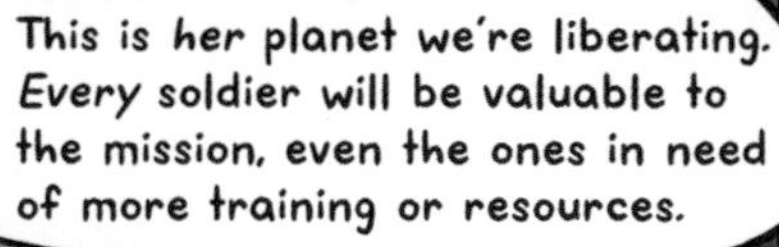
This is *her* planet we're liberating. *Every* soldier will be valuable to the mission, even the ones in need of more training or resources.

We don't have any resources to *waste* right now. Those suits, especially. They're more valuable than almost any soldier we could put them on.

Have I ever asked for *anything* without proving to you how valuable I can be?
Of course not. You've always gotten the job done. But the Empire's been hitting us *hard* ever since you took those suits.

KRRMMBL
We need to hit just as hard. No weakness, no failures.

Hey, stranger! What's that weird smell on you?
They filled up a pool for us at the warehouse. Zero-gee training.

How'd you get that much *water?*
It was gray water.
*Gross.* No wonder you smell like a toilet.

I'm almost done filling your prescriptions. Hand me your fancy card?
They must be paying you good now. This is a *lot.*
Some of the meds are new. Is this everything?

Nope, there's shortages. Empire crawling up our butt and all.
Yeah.
You're lucky you're high enough priority to get *anything* for cramps.
. . . yeah.

Hey, c'mon. Glad you got your wish, kid.
Knock 'em dead!

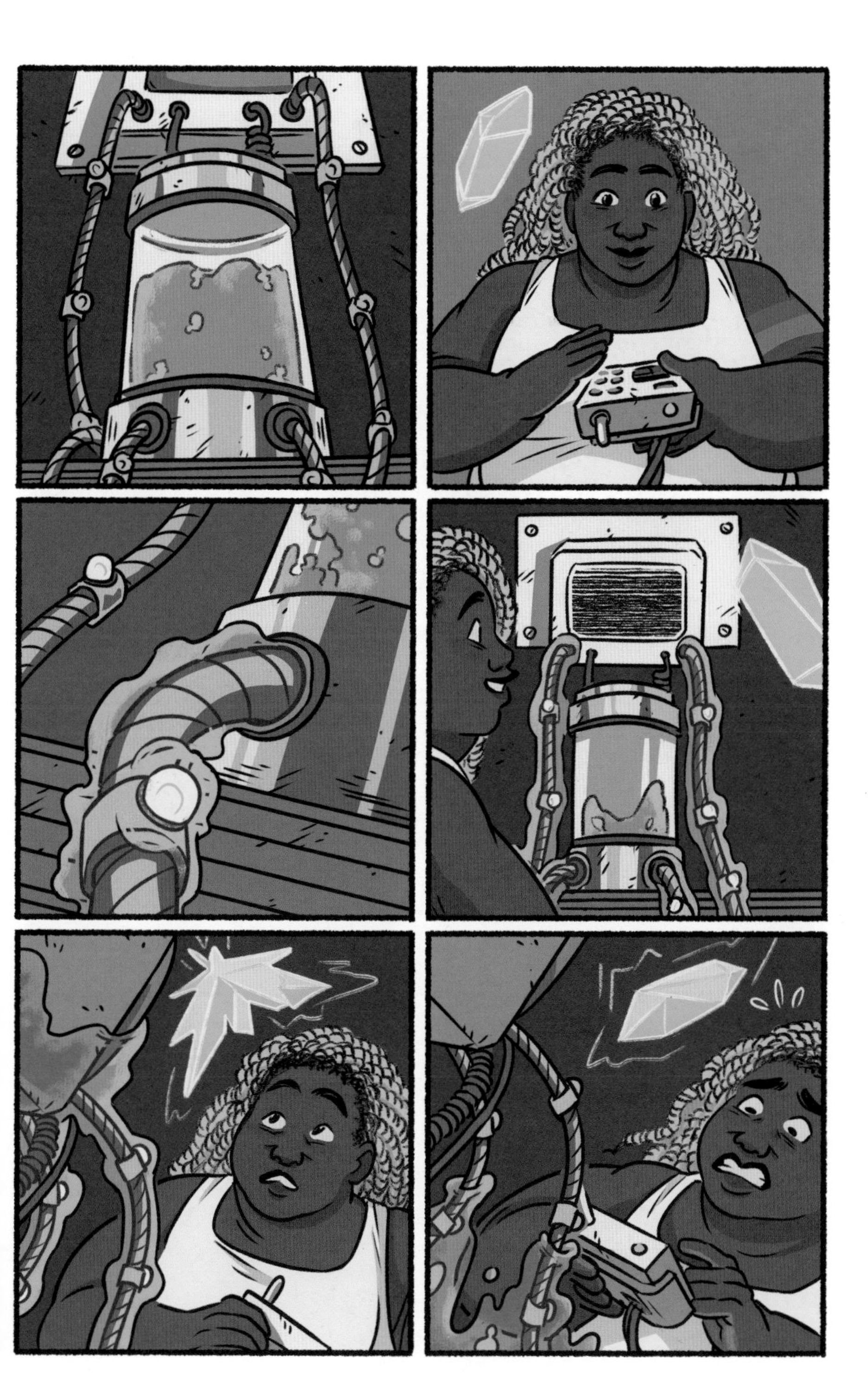

Young guest! Got a minute?

How can I help?
This server's going into the wall. Help me lift?

Two . . . three! There we go. Hand me the connectors.
I swear, installing a new server's always a hassle.

Hey, Daari – Dngal's your kid, right? The oldest one out in the square?
Mm-hm.

She's got a real head for machines. She ever help you out with these installations?
No, this is war effort stuff. No place for kids.

I don't understand. She's, like, *twelve*. She's not that little.

In the valleys, only adults can choose to collaborate with the Firebacks.
We try to give our children as normal of a childhood as we can.
Afternoon, cousin. Where are you heading today?
Ibben. Their fabricators need replacement parts.
The people have been running them day and night to repair the damage from yesterday's Empire strike. They've asked for help.
Another valley town got attacked? Didn't our counterstrike unit help fend it off?
The Firebacks . . . show friendship by fighting our shared enemy. But when you invite such friends to your house, cousin, do they ever *leave*?
Shush.
Ruust, lend me a hand.
Uh – yes, Sarge! Excuse me, Daari.
Other way.
The palm faces the other way.
Oh – oh no. What was I doing?
*It involves defecation.*

Okay, gotta go goodbye–
Ahahaha, Sertig! You just ruined the best joke in town!
Is that everything?
Yes, thank you.
This equipment . . . Did you bring all of this up from the base?
Does Nide know–?
Why don't you ride along to Ibben with me?
It's not far. You probably cover more distance on your jogs.

Okay, so I've conducted more tests . . .

. . . based on the hypothesis that the goo is an *energy medium* of some kind.
I scavenged some old tech and connected it to my setup . . .
MWEHHH
MWEHH

. . . and it activated everything! It even made a go at Field's local power conduit!
I can't say I cared for the experience.

It's definitely designed to interface with technology as well as the neural impulses of the wearer. Just keep that in mind when they let you wear the suit again, okay?

*You're* the one in control.

Today's the day, squad. Suit up.
Our tireless techs have figured out that the armor can respond to the thoughts of whoever's wearing it. So you'll be the ones in the pilot seats today.

Instruct your armor to activate.

hh-
GLP

hhh-

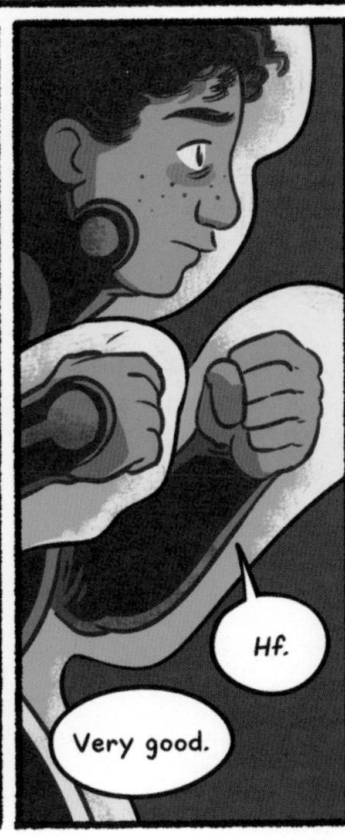
Hf.
Very good.

Our tireless techs have *also* worked on a few fun surprises for your training today.

And these surprises are following their own instructions.

KRINKRINKRIN

KCHUNK KCHUNK
KCHUNK KCHUN
Meet the training drones, built from Blossom scraps.
KCHUNK
Our enemy oppresses freedom around the galaxy by using cold, soulless machines . . .

. . . and it's our duty to dismantle them before they dismantle us.
Begin.

Gah!
WHK
GRNK
WHF
Ha-
GLP
GRNCH

GLG
C'mon–
glg glg glg
KRNNN
Show it who's boss!
KRNNN
Fassen! Quit playing defense!

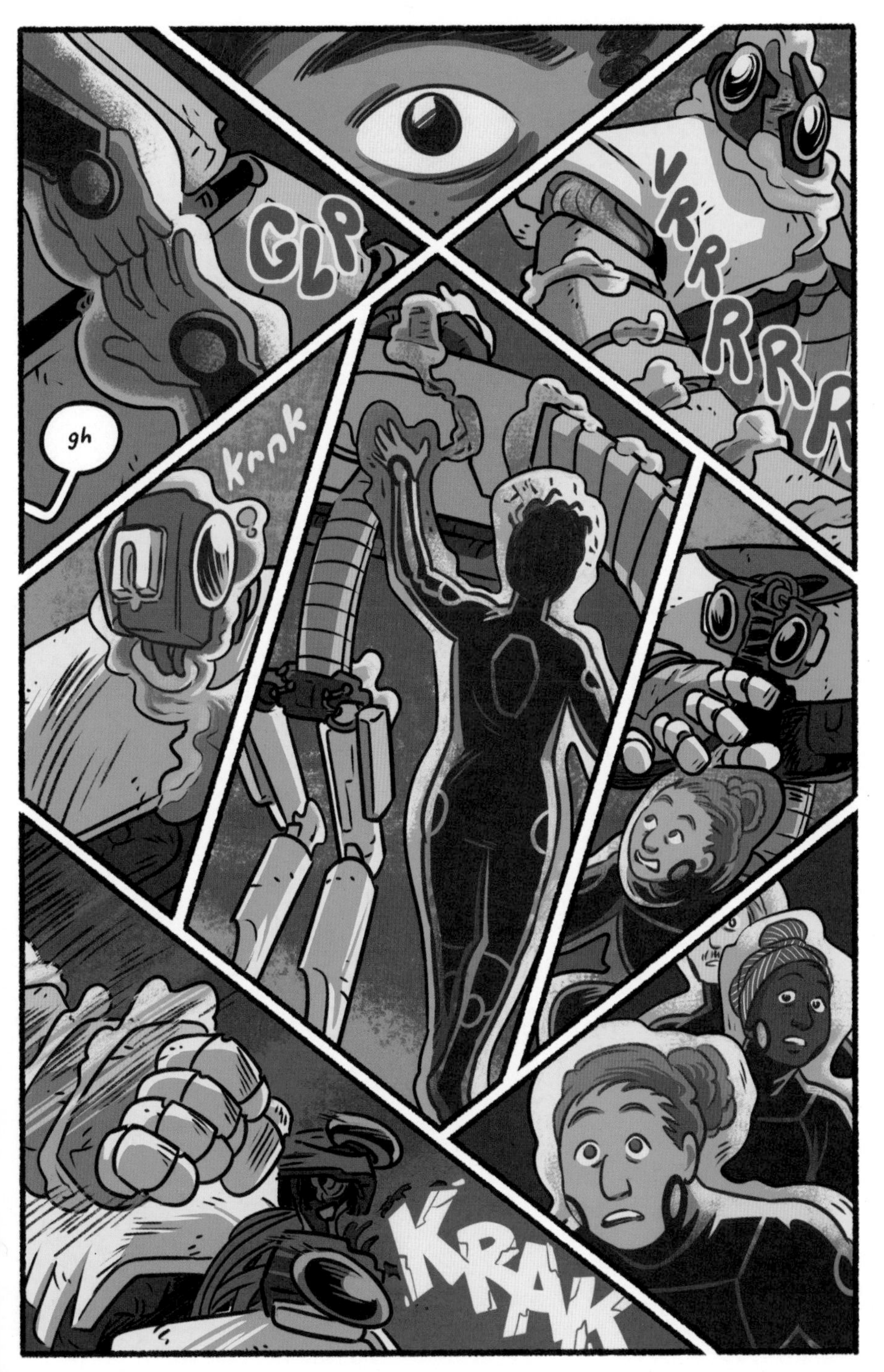
GLP
VRRRRRR
gh
krnk
KRAK

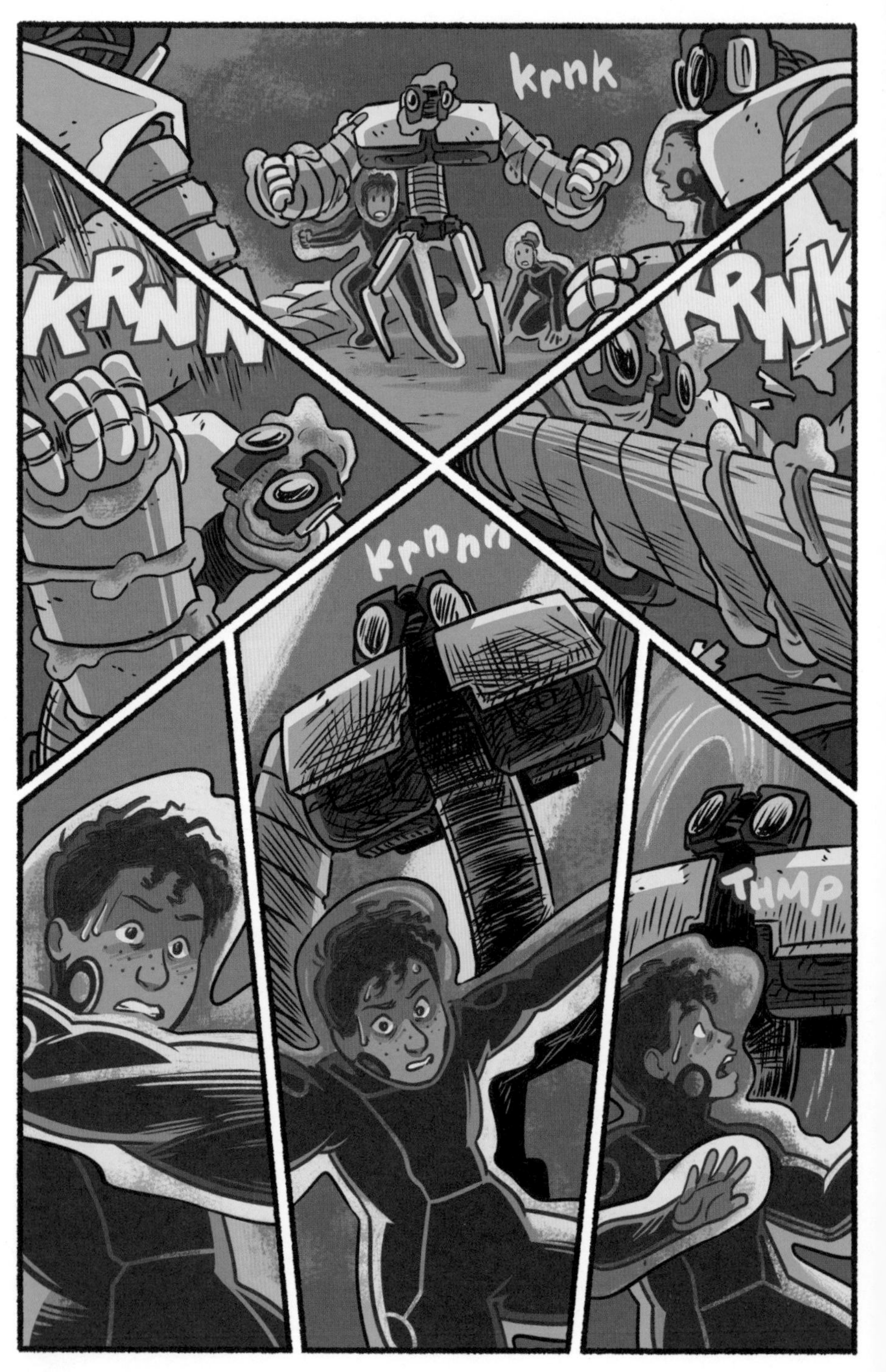
krnk
KRNN
KRNK
krnnn
THMP

g'k
SKRI
IIIK
glp
Show everyone exactly how you did that.

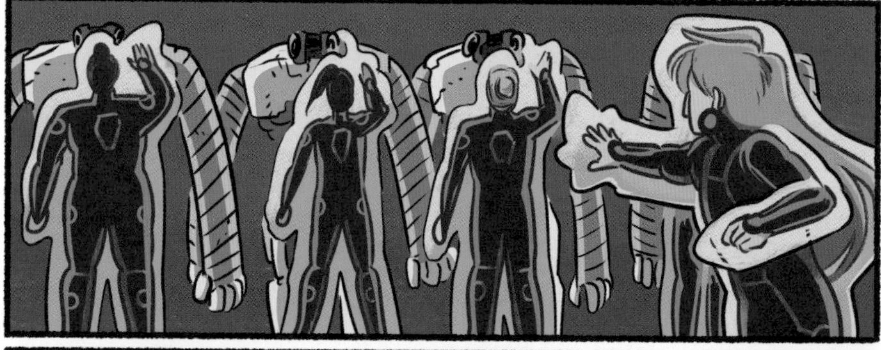

KOF
At ease! We're done for the day. Go see the techs for suit removal.

Captain Lumen, a minute?
Nide's fine, kid. What's up?
How'd you make the sword?

SHLP
Oh, easy! I'll show ya.
SHLP
Get into your stance and focus on your dominant hand. You a lefty?
Uh-huh.

Strengthen your armor to a point. You don't want size. You want *sharpness.*

KLAK
Ah!
Stay focused! And fight back! And have some *style!*
KLAK
KLAK

HA-
glp

Excellent! You're full of-
-surprises!

Now let's-
-take a-

Nide? Captain?
WHUMP

I killed him oh no oh no
'll be court-martialed fo
this I reall ed Nide

Airway.
Check his airway.

Pulse—
The hell are you doing?

Th-the captain just collapsed—
Was he injured?
I didn't hit him!

Was he having trouble breathing?
I—
Yeah.

I thought it might've been a heart attack. I-
Bekko. Avet.

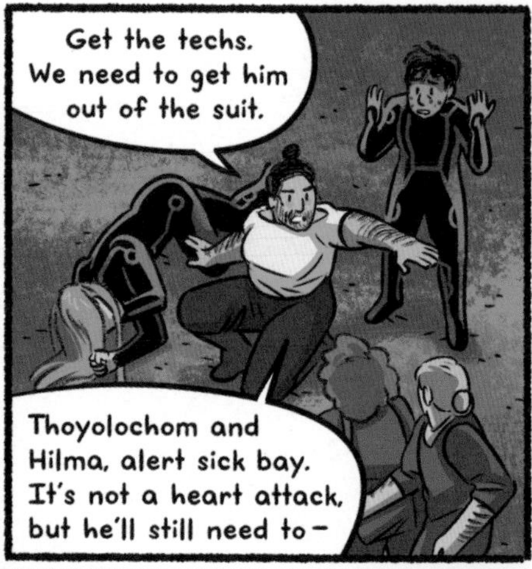
Get the techs. We need to get him out of the suit.
Thoyolochom and Hilma, alert sick bay. It's not a heart attack, but he'll still need to-

Drink some water.

He's doing well. It's good you were the closest when he fainted.
Th-thanks.

Avet and Bekko are good in a fight but I wouldn't trust them to tell the difference between sunstroke and a stomachache.
INSERT PAYMENT
You have medical training, too? I thought you were a fighter from the start.

Those of us from the valleys don't distinguish between healers and fighters so sharply as you from off-planet do.

PAYME
You mean the Firebacks?
BDA
GR SERTIG
SGT 19942-39
I mean *all* of you.

The Empire also segregates people based on their assigned duties.
You fight their tyranny and yet you hold on to that tradition without thinking.
I warned you, twelve hours is the *maximum.* No more.
If this keeps happening, as a physician . . .

Oh, come on, don't pull rank on m
—may have to advise the generals that your . . . *health issues* make you unfit to lead this mission—
EXCUSE ME?!

I've spent *fifteen years* dragging Blossom crap back here for them to use. They'd be squatting in an *empty hole* if it weren't for me.
Are you really gonna *ground* me for telling you what I *need?*

I'm gonna wear that binder under the suit, and I'm gonna take that cargo ship down with my squad.

I'm gonna bring that colony to its *knees.* And I'll do it in *twelve hours* if I have to.

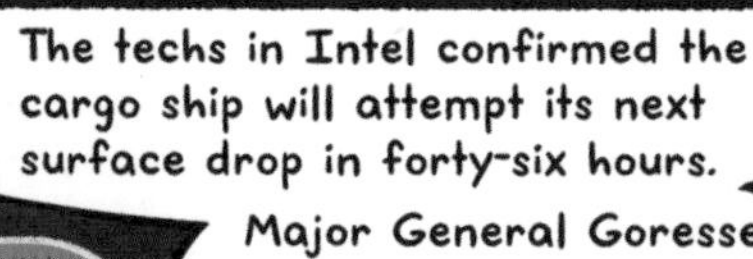
The techs in Intel confirmed the cargo ship will attempt its next surface drop in forty-six hours.
Major General Goresse is mobilizing all air units to support the operation.

I bet you're all sick of the Empire stomping upstairs while we're trying to sleep, huh?

Yes, Captain!
That's what I thought. Get some shut-eye, squad. We'll review our mission tomorrow. Dismissed.

You're giving me déjà vu, Fassen.
I was just curious if you were feeling better, Captain.
Nide.
Captain.

Aw, no sweat. Just taking it easy so the doc doesn't fuss over me.

Any other questions?

The thing you need to wear under the suit. Is it for your . . .
chest?
Sir?

You wear one?
No, um, I mean—
—do you wear it all the time?

Usually, no. But that Blossom suit is damn formfitting.
That's the nice thing about the usual uniform, it hides a lot. And you can decorate it with any trophies you knock off the drones.

Do you know why we collect these souvenirs, Fassen?
It's a tradition. Taking pride in doing your duty.
Sure, there's pride. There's glory. But it's also a *reminder.*

We've *earned* whatever we take. We've *earned* the best food in the mess. Especially when the supplies run short and the lines run long.

And not just the food lines, either. Am I right, medic?
I read about the stuff that changes your body and your voice. It shows up in supplies sometimes, but . . .

. . . it's hard to get.
Yeah. You gotta fight just as hard for *hormones* as you do for *freedom*. But it gets easier the higher you climb.
THE ONLY WAY TO VICTORY!
I have a fabric ration under my name I haven't used yet.

Let me know if it would come in handy.
Okay.

Th- thank you.
ONLY W
VICTORY

Glad to be of service, kid.

Ruust!
Good luck tomorrow, Ruust!
Krak
krakl
Perfect.
BWEEP

Fassen!
Good morning!

It's almost sunset here, Lu. But it's good to see you, too.

Yeah. Your hair's the longest I've ever seen it!

And you've gotten more muscles, too.
Is that from training?

Hahahaha!
Yeah, probably!
Hey, Lu, listen—

Those coordinates I gave you last time—did you figure out what channel they'd fall in?
I did, but—
You know those coordinates aren't on Tsanggho, right? They're barely in the same *solar system.*

Yeah, well, um. I've been briefed on the squad's first mission and . . .
. . . and it takes us a bit farther from home than I expected.

You're leaving for your first mission?

Why didn't you *tell* me?
Oh dear.

I'm sorry, Lu. It all happened really fast. Our mission depends on the cargo ship schedule that Intel scrapes off the Blossom channels.

But it's still local, okay? We're helping our base deal with a supply problem.
Warfare sounds so much simpler when you're merely "dealing with a problem."

But our *schedule*! Who knows when I'll get to talk to you again?

We can keep our schedule, Lu. That's why I gave you the new coordinates. I'll find a way to sneak off and talk to you. I always have.

No, but—
The tests—

I haven't finished the test on the armor substance. I can't—

I won't be able to help you if you . . .

What if something happens to you?

Lu . . .

Listen, Lu . . .

You said you looked up the matching channel for the new coordinates.
Where will you need to go if you wanna talk to me?
snf
Oh, um. Actually, that part's really cool. The radiation in this particular channel is only released by certain stellar phenomena.

Wait, hold on. I'll show you.
I think I'll fly us to . . .

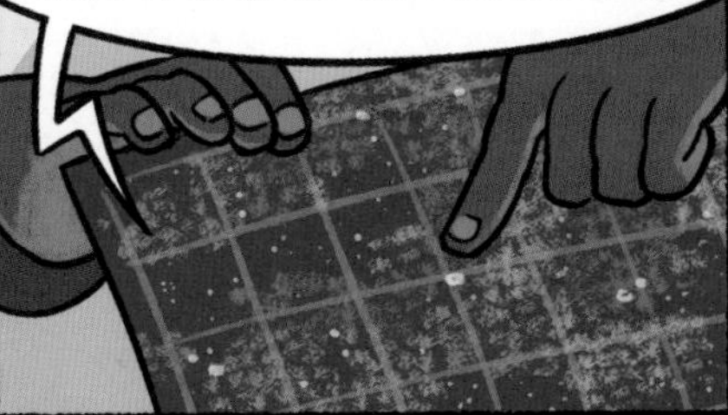
. . . this band of the channel here. See this spot? From here I'll be able to view an incredible nebula.

Field's told me about what I would see. It's not very poetic when it comes to describing colors, but the nebula sounds *beautiful.*

krik
krak

Hey, listen, I should go. I've still got a curfew and I don't want anyone thinking I've deserted.

Okay. Fassen . . .
. . . be safe, okay? Take care of yourself.
I will. Thank you, Lu. I'll message you when I can.
CALL DISCONNECTED
BWEEP

Target approaching on schedule.
It's making its deliveries. Call in when we have escort visuals.

Roger, control.

VRRRRRRRR

Escort ships have been detected.

Green squadron, red squadron, move in.
Roger.

Targets are within range!
Cloud formation!
VRRR
PCHAK
VRRRR
PCHAK
Black squadron, acknowledge.
That's our cue. Don't fly too fancy.
PCHAK
VRRR
PCHAK

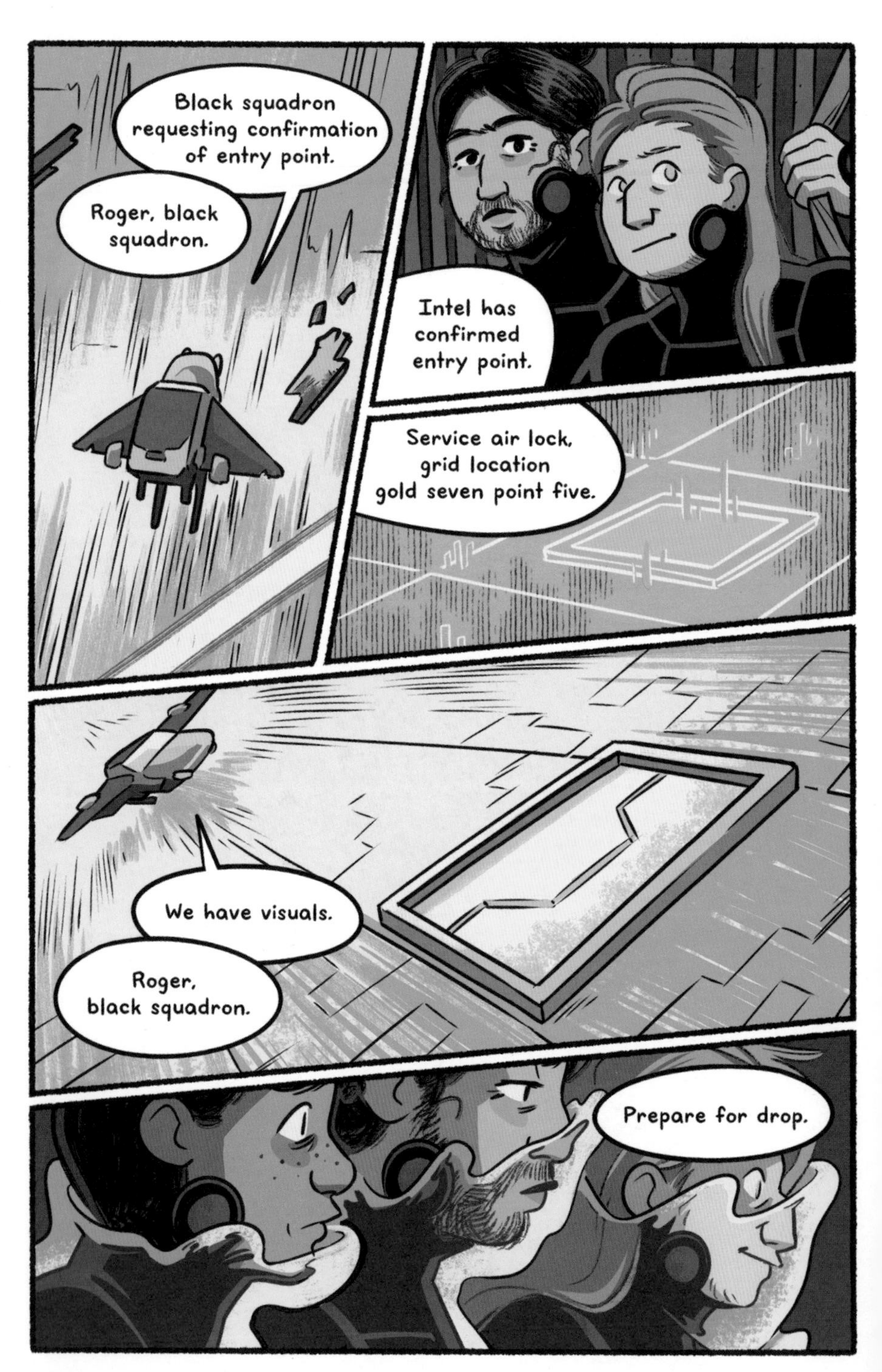
Black squadron requesting confirmation of entry point.
Roger, black squadron.
Intel has confirmed entry point.
Service air lock, grid location gold seven point five.
We have visuals.
Roger, black squadron.
Prepare for drop.

Opening hatch. Commence drop in T-minus five . . . four . . . three . . .
Two . . . one.
THMP
Sound off! One!
Two!
Three.
Four.
Five!
S-six.
Seven.
Eight!
Black squadron drop successful!

Black ship returning to formation. Have a nice flight, Captain.
All squadrons commence next phase, anti-deployment fire.
Hang tight, kids.
Roger. All squadrons firing.
We have rising altitude. Target has retreated from deployment position.
Good! Keep firing. Make 'em leave!
VVVVVVVR

RRRRRRrrrrr

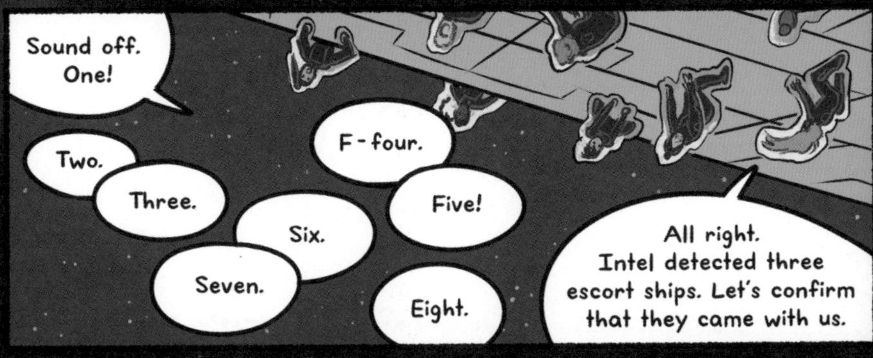
Sound off. One!
Two.
Three.
F-four.
Five!
Six.
Seven.
Eight.
All right. Intel detected three escort ships. Let's confirm that they came with us.

Escort one confirmed.
Escort two and three confirmed. One's doing a sweep, but the other one's starting its dock sequence.
Great. Let's not give them anything to find.
We'll let ourselves in.
Got it, Avet?
Roger.
It's heavy.
Don't worry 'bout the mess. It'll look like battle damage to anyone doing a sweep.

Got it!
krrrr
Got atmo.
Got gravity, too.
Yep, this is the primary service tunnel. Intel got that right, too.
This is the spine of the ship. Bridge is at the head.
Check all the vents and corners.

Captain! These vents look down into the docking bay!
Escort two's docked.
Roger. How about the other docking bays?
Docking bay one's occupied, too.
We've got number three pulling in here.
There's a fourth bay on this side that's unoccupied. Not a lot of free floor space, though.
Intel said three. They might be using that one for storage. Speaking of which—

Here's the cargo hold.
Are you kidding me?

I've seen warehouses smaller than this.
Vehicles, tools—
Food rations.

SWIV
Sssh!
What's—

KCHUNK

KCHAK

Robots.
Yech. They don't get any less creepy, do they?
Where's the crew?

That's what the Empire's so proud of.

Machines running everybody's lives. Devouring worlds. Devouring people.
Squeezing them into easy convenient shapes.

Roger, Captain. But where are the people? There are soldiers on all the convoys.
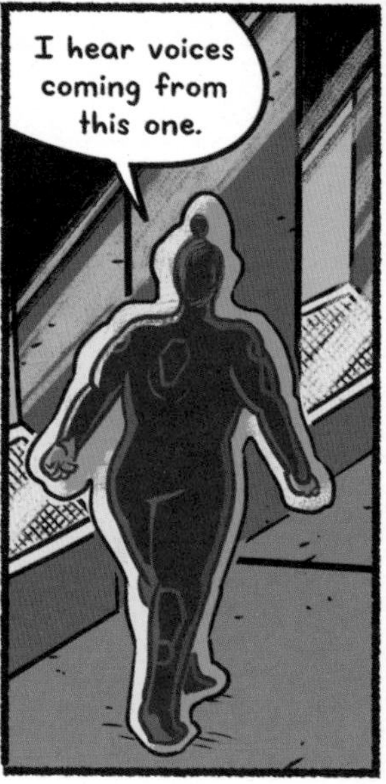
I hear voices coming from this one.
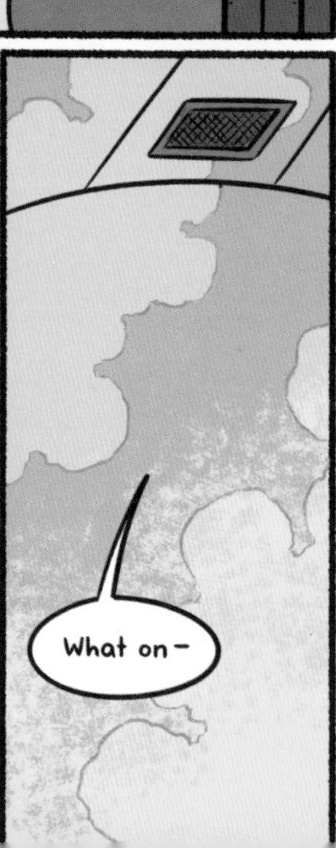
What on—

Barracks?
No, they're not all soldiers, look.

Civilians. Pretty fancy, too, see? Retainers and everything.
They actually *dress* like that?

There are *children!*
Why are there such young children on a *supply ship?*

Those colonists must be valued pretty highly if they can request their *families* along with their supplies.

My family already *lives* here! My cousins have to face firefights and bombardments every day! They *chose* to drag children here?
They *chose* to drag children into the mess they made?
They didn't expect this much Fireback resistance. The Empire's used to getting their way.

They don't care about your family. They want your planet. And we won't let them have it.
Right.
Right.

One at the helm, one on machine supervision, one on comms, and one on security. If we focus on those last two—

Comms, yes, but we need to control the machine station as soon as possible The human crew's small enough for us to handle if the robots don't fuss.

Bekko and Avet, you're fastest. Sneak through the vents and take out those two stations. Sertig, subdue the captain before they can override any protocols themself.
Hilma, disarm the crew and hand off their weapons to Thoyolochom—
KCHAK
SWIV
PSH
SWIV
gh—
glip
I got it! Should I destroy it?

Just a sec. We can work with this.

Well, tell them we'll be *delayed.* They can survive another day in the hab section.

Any word from—
thmp
WHSH
KCHAK
CHAK
What—

GAH-
Captain!
WHMP
THWAK
AGH!
gf -!
This is a nice little ship, Captain.
I think we'll put it to good use.

Attention, passengers and crew. An evacuation is in effect.
Atmosphere has been depleted in sections one through six.
Atmosphere has been depleted in sections seven through twelve.
Please remain calm.

Please proceed to the –

Hilma, you okay?
That thing did something to my suit. I can't activate my armor anymore!

Stay near me in case we lose atmo.

Keep moving, Captain. Didn't you hear the announcement?

Please remain calm.

going on?
Let us go!
aboard?
scum
trapped

This is what took out your armor, Hilma?

That's right. Cut through it like jelly and zapped my suit.
I—I don't know how much help I'll be without it . . .

There's still enough of us to make do. Just don't get in the way.
The rest of you, keep your armor at least fifty millimeters thick at all points.

No more surprises.

N-Nide?
There's another ship.

Say again?
There's another escort ship! See?

Is *that* why this bay was empty?
No way. Intel picked up every signal in Tsanggho orbit. There wasn't anything else this close. The nearest Blossom ships are almost a day's trip away!
Well, it can't be a *ghost*—

You people don't *know*?
But you're wearing— You have *no* idea?

Talkative, are we? Why don't you enlighten us?
The hell did it go?!
You lost it?
Lost nothing! It *disappeared!*
It's true. I was watching it, too.
Wait – *wait!* There it is, upper right quadrant!
How's it sneaking around that fast?
Unbelievable. They actually made one.
It's a *jumpship.*
What?
That ship's not just fast. It jumps between points in space . . .
. . . *instantaneously.*
Right, Captain?

But that's faster than anything other than . . . broadcasts! Channel messages! You can't do that with . . . with *stuff!*
*That* thing can.

That's what's so special about that shipyard they're trying to build here, huh, Captain? That's why the colonists get to have their families here. You wanna treat them nice.

They're gonna make *more* of those things for you.
Oh, we struck *freshwater* today.

And these suits have something to do with them?
You'll get nothing more from me.

Oh, I think we will. One way or another, you'll get us that ship.
Nide!

I have an idea!

thmp

Here's the captain's comm, but it's got a biometric lock on it.
Biometric, huh?

So what do we gotta extract from you to access the jump-ship's call signal? DNA? Fingerprints?
. . .
Sertig, help me figure out exactly what we need to *extract.*

There we go – evacuation order, return to docking bay ASAP. Aaaaand, transmit.

And look at that. Our jumpship's coming in now.

There, Captain, isn't it easier to cooperate?

hh
hh

hf

KRNK
What the–
Who are you?
Hull breach detected.

You're a Fireback?
You're a pilot?
Get out of my ship!
GLP
Gh-
GWSH
Gorge preset three.

VVVRRRR
KRRRRR

Where are-
Where'd you-
No!
Oh no no no no-
I can't stay here-
Take me back!
Last coordinates!
Go back!
Back!

BAM
krnk
AAAAAAAAAA
AAAA
AAAAA
AAAA
AUGH
EEEA

tink
Fassen!
THMP
You okay?
Y-yeah. Nide, that—
That thing doesn't move like any ship I've ever seen.
When it disappears it dives into some kind of—of weird *subspace.*
These suits help the pilots survive the jump and control the ship! Nide, this changes *everything!*

Understatement of the decade!
Squad! Cadet Ruust just ensured our legacy in the fight for freedom!

We didn't just win a cargo ship – we secured cutting-edge technology that will change how we fight the Empire!
How we *win!*

There's only one loose end for us to tie up. Scoot those prisoners over to the wall . . .

. . . and shoot them out the air lock.

Wh-what?

All right, to the wall.
No!
Our parents are waiting for us down there!
Wait a minute! Wait a minute!

Wait! What? Nide, most of the prisoners are *civilians!*

Can't we separate them from the soldiers?

They're *all* Blossom, Fassen. You think those *colonists* oppress us any less than the crew?

Fassen, c'mon, we need you on the line. They're starting to squirm.
What about the *kids*, Nide?
There are babies that were probably born on the way *here!* They didn't sign up for this!
Kid, I know they pulled you outta your civics class early, but this is basic stuff.
Living in an unjust system makes them unjust. Letting these kids go means letting them inherit the Empire that *attacks* us every day.
The Empire that *orphaned* you.

These kids aren't like you, Fassen. They don't know how to do the right thing. Those kids are gonna make Tsanggho their *playground* because their parents said they could.

There's got to be a way for us to win this without *killing them!*

Take them back to the base! Tell the Empire we'll let them go if the valley bombardments stop! *Anything else!*

*Cadet.*
This isn't cute anymore. And it's not *useful.*

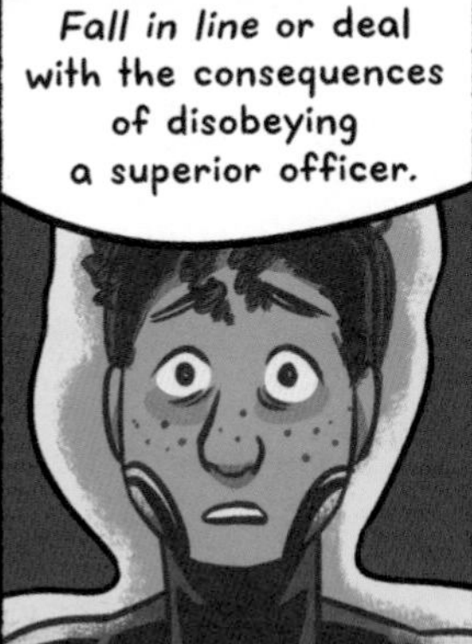
*Fall in line* or deal with the consequences of disobeying a superior officer.

. . .
I-
Atmosphere restored in Docking Bay 3.

PSHHHHH

Second lieutenant!
Now! Push the barrier!
ZZT
GLSH
All hands!
All hands on the crew!
What's happening?
C'mon!
There's a ship in the next docking bay! Grab the kids! We might lose atmo again!

Fassen!
Hilma!
They boarding ship number three? Lemme pilot it back to base. Not like I can do much good back there.
But — you disobeyed orders, too! You'll be punished for disrupting the mission!
The mission went to pot the second that crazy thing got lodged in the hull. I didn't train to jettison kids into space. Did you?
These kids'll have a better chance at the base than they will floating around out there.
Besides . . .
. . . I didn't throw up on the zero-gee simulator, either. I can get us to the ground no problem.

Th-thank you.
Go round up any stragglers.

I have to admit—
I liked your *last* idea much better than *this* one.
LAUNCH! LAUNCH NOW!

VRRRRR
Nide–
I thought you understood how this works, Fassen. Insubordination is not an option. Anything other than a total victory is not an option. It makes us *look bad.* It makes *me* look bad.
Know what *else* makes me look bad?
GSH
Wasting my time on some soft *nobody* because I thought I saw some *potential.*
GLK

GWSH
SWP
KLAK
hn
GRK

Sertig. What are you *doing*.
They just sent a ship of *invaders* on through to your planet.
Don't pretend you're doing this for *my* sake. You're doing this because Fassen made you look *weak*.
I know how you get when someone stands in the way of something you want.
So what will you do about me?
hf
SCRP
SCRP
Don't do *this*.
Sertig, don't *do* this—
Out.

Get me out, get me out, get me out!
VVVRRR
KREEEE
AH!
hh
Don't—
Don't close your eyes—
Don't close your eyes—

Where-
ZIP
Where can I go?
SEARCHING...
CHANNEL DETECTED.
Where are you?
Lu-
Where will you be?
Please-
-get me out of here!

Take me to Lu!

's a snack
or when you're
past the border.
Don't be gone
too long, dear.

Is everything all right?

Uh-huh. Totally. Just running a diagnostic on the engine.
You ran one this morning.

The propulsion feels a little laggy. Can you check the ionization levels?
If you insist.

But I am perfectly capable of sustaining a conversation in the meantime.
And until Fassen calls, I'm the only one you can talk to.
Sigh

I just wish I knew if they were all right.
I wish I could tell you if they were. But I can't. I'm sorry.
Why don't you have one of your aunt's cookies?

I know you like hers more than mine.
Mm.
It's true. Why do hers always taste better?

Because she frets over you, and that makes her do even better at what she's already good at.
You should try on that elaborate sweater while you're at it.

Mmmmm. I dunno. Is it as itchy as the last one she made?
You'll have to be the judge of—
—that.

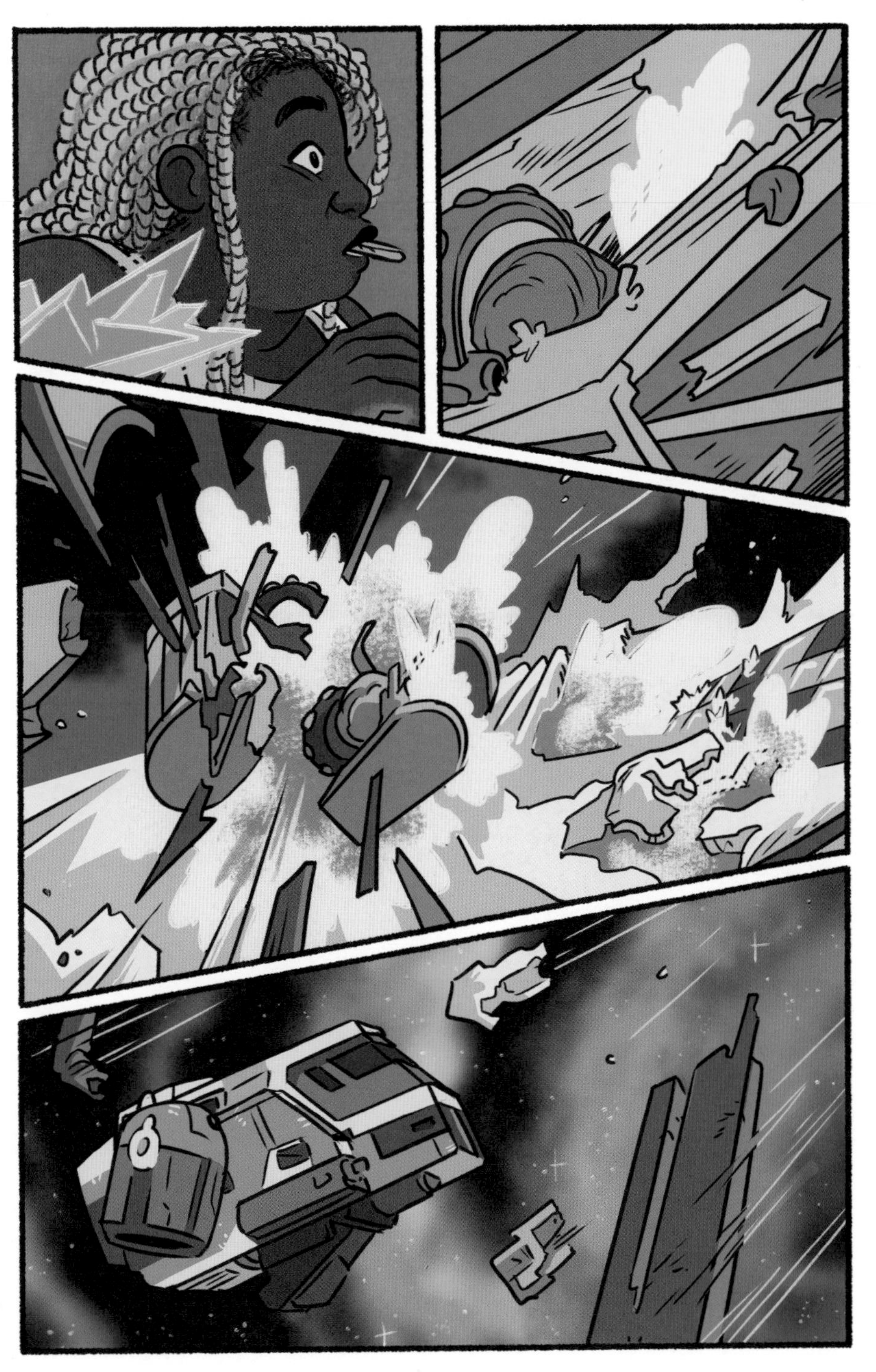

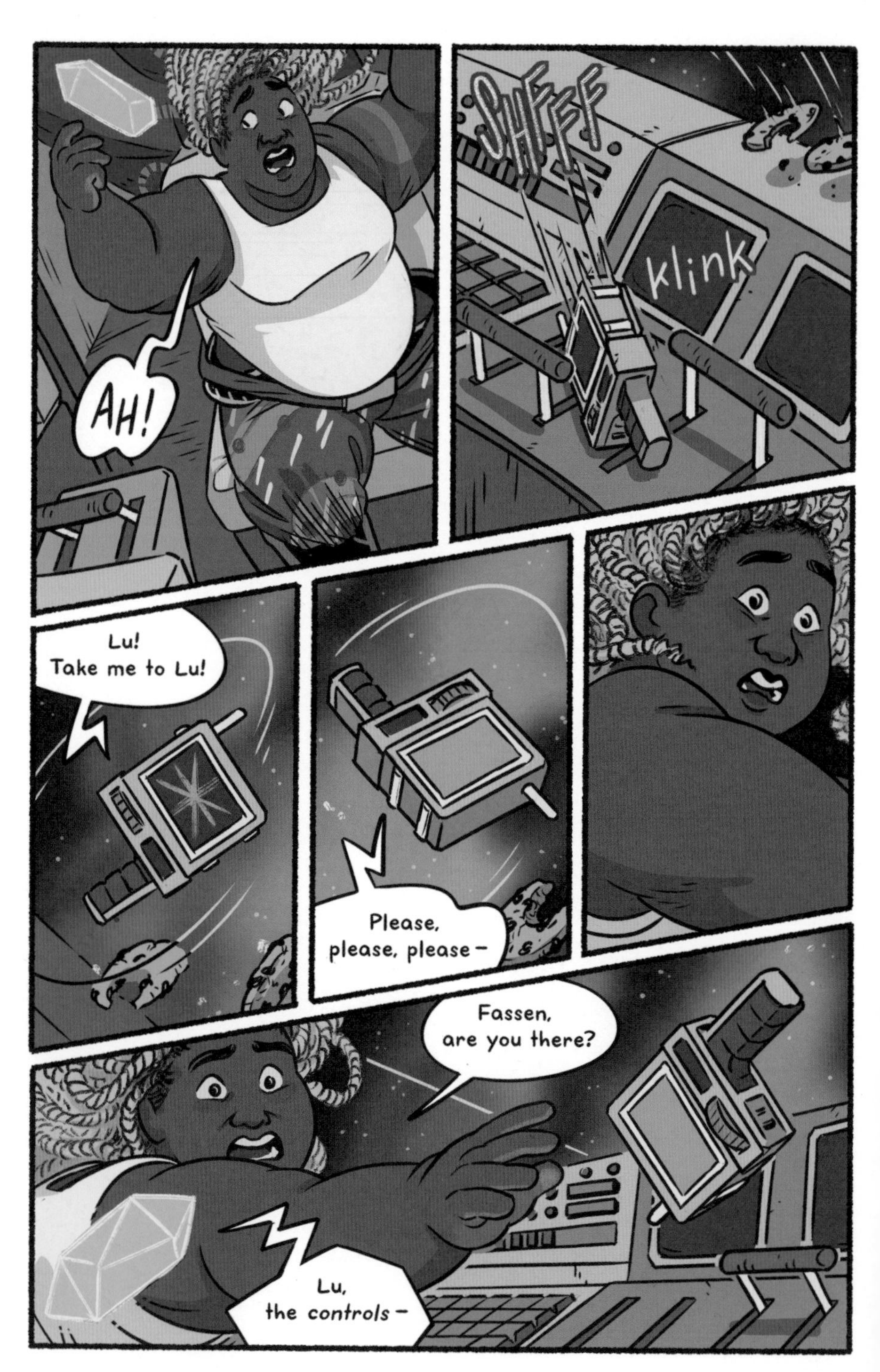
AH!
SHFFF
klink
Lu!
Take me to Lu!
Please,
please, please–
Fassen,
are you there?
Lu,
the controls–

Fassen? Fassen, it's me!
Something's happened over here. A ship just appeared and *exploded*–
That was me! I'm at the coordinates you gave me!
Wh-what? *How?!* You're, like, fifty light-years away!
It's– it's a long story.
If you were on the fastest ship in the Empire, that would take–
fifty lights, carry the two
–eighty days? *Ninety?*
Lu, the *debris*–
I promise I'll explain. I just–
I need you to find me. I'm in the wreck. I–

Sergeant?
Hold on, Lu. Sergeant?
Ohhh no okay okay okay–
Sergeant!
Fassen? What's going on?
One of my squadmates got pinned to the ship–
C'mon, c'mon, c'mon–

I'm closing in on your signal. Is that you in the suit? On that – what *kind* of ship is that, anyway?
Lu, I –
I can't get my squadmate out. Can you help?
Lu –
I *know* you don't like it, Field!
That thing's torn to shreds. Maybe I can help pull –
tink
Lu –
tip tap tip
tip
TONK
TONK
TONK
tink

AAAHH!
Fassen!
Nnh!
Lu!
It broke off!
Maybe I can–
Lu!
This is a very bad idea!

FLIP
FLIP
KRRRM
FFFSSSH
BROOM

KLANG
KRATTL
RRRMBLE
Nnn
Hh
hh
KLAK
KLAK
Sergeant?

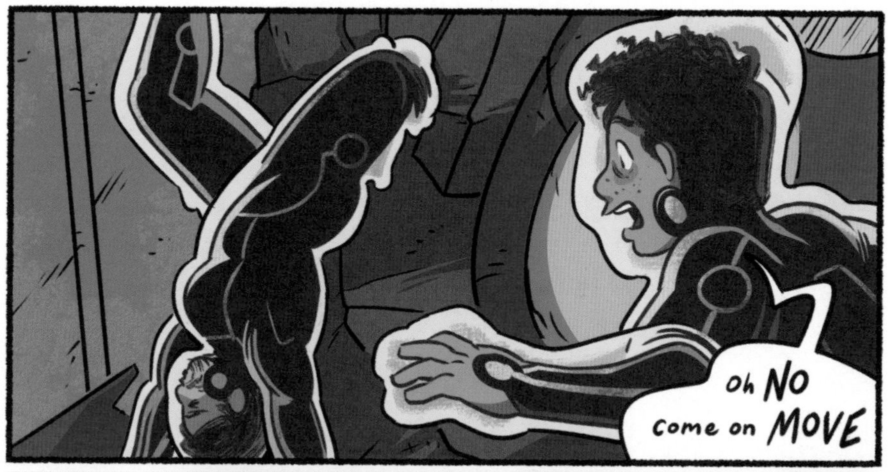
Oh NO
come on MOVE

COME. ON.
KRRR

KRRAAANCH
Fassen?

THMP

WHFFF

Fassen!

GL
SH

Oh, Fassen!

I'm so glad you're all right! How is this *happening*?

Sergeant–

My squadmate, she–
–she's hurt real bad.

I gotta find out how bad her . . .

. . . her . . .
Hold on!

What do I do?
Roll them on their side. Let me look at the other one.

We'll stabilize her and then we need to get the ship out of here as soon as

Hh

FASSEN

How do you switch from gray water to fresh water?

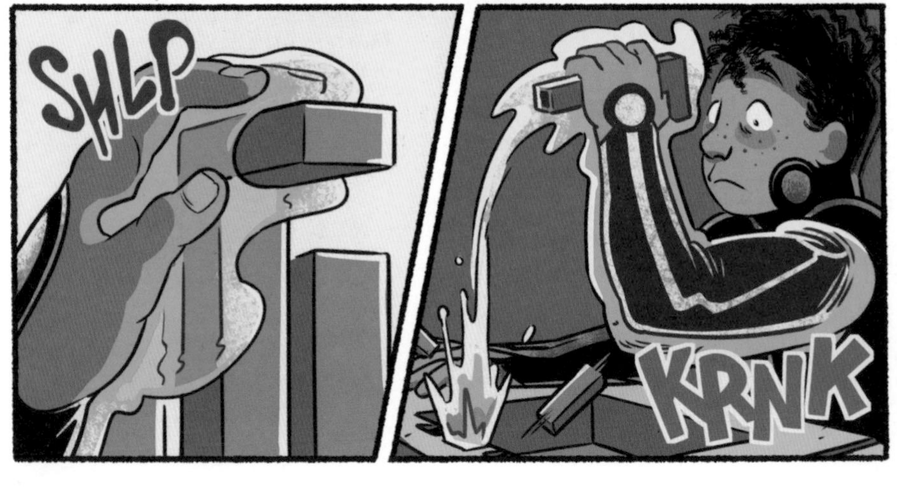
SHLP
KRNK

BLOSH

Oh no no no

Well, they're awake.
Fassen!

Good, you're up!
BLSH

I-I-
I'm so sorry. That was so much water—
No worries. Hand me the faucet?

There we go. You want some tea?
S-sure.

How's your friend? The armor seems to have stabilized her.

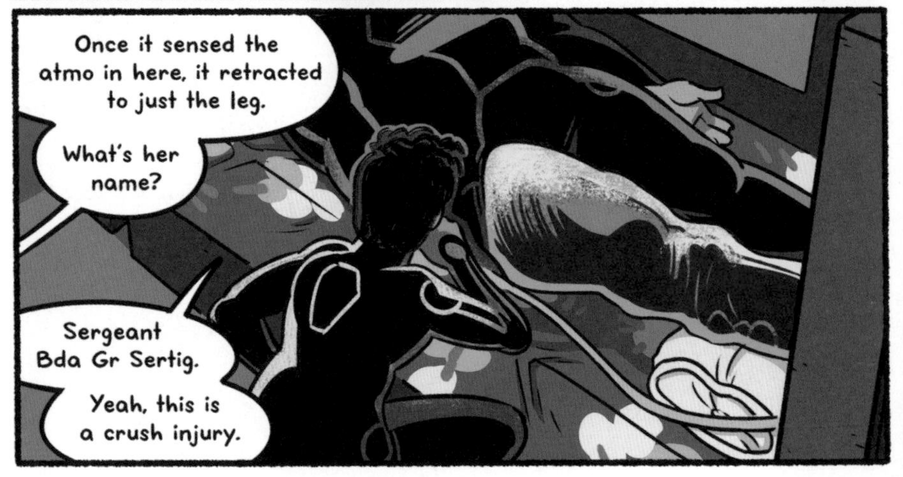
Once it sensed the atmo in here, it retracted to just the leg.
What's her name?
Sergeant Bda Gr Sertig.
Yeah, this is a crush injury.

You used a medkit on her, right? Can I have it?
One second.
I see. The suit is compressing her leg to protect her.
Uh-huh. It's keeping most of the toxins that were released by the injured tissue out of her system.
Fluids'll help but . . .

Eventually she'll need a real doctor to look at her.

Field'll keep an eye on her. Come up to the cockpit with me.

I didn't have a *plan* in mind coming out here. I just . . . *wanted* it. And the ship listened.

But that in-between place – it didn't even feel like a *place.* It felt like it was squeezing me into *nothing.*

I just had to be anywhere else. I-I couldn't be there anymore.
This explains the wreck we found, Lu. If this instantaneous travel is a new development, we may have come across a test ship.

This could change everything for the Empire. If they can transmit a *warship* as quickly as a message –

That settles it.

We're taking you back to the commune.
Lu-
No, listen!

We know what the suits are for now! We have to study them more. And that'll help you keep the commune away from the Empire, right?

And Fassen, you and Sertig traveled at least fifty light-years to get away. Both the Empire and the Firebacks'll go after you if you try to return home.
But-

*Therefore*, they are both eligible for consideration as residents of the Field Commune. Right, Field?

Of all the—
—*mental gymnastics* you've thrust upon me—

—over the course of your dealings with this—this *troublemaker*—

—of all the *appeals* and the *half truths* and the *technicalities*—

—this is the most technically correct.
Having fled an Imperial expansionist action and traveled into distant neutral space, they are both welcome to enter the commune unless their presence provokes any response from the Empire.

And we're not gonna tell any stories to make anyone think the Empire is interested in them, are we, Field?
I love you, Lu, but you are a *terror*.

Okay, now we . . .

. . . just need to make sure we all agree on the story we're going to tell.

How 'bout you tell us more about the two-person houseboat we pulled you out of after it suffered a catastrophic hull breach?
What was it called again? The *Quickbread?*

They're all so . . . different.
Uh-huh. Once in a while we get someone new, fleeing from Blossom expansion.
But it's hard to find us if you don't know where to look. We're pretty far out.
ZZZT
We've reentered Field space.
And your aunt has wasted no time in calling you.

K THUNK

Was that Sertig?
She's coming too. Hold on.

What happened?! Where—
Shhh!!! It's me! It's okay!

Trust me. You've been hurt. We're going somewhere we can treat you.

We just . . . gotta cover some stuff first, okay?

Lu, she's waiting.
I'll take it.

Hi, Auntie Bo!
Is everything all right? You were supposed to be back yesterday morning!

An independent settlement?
Uh-huh.
They don't like the Empire any more than we do. They just don't like *soldiers*, either, no matter what the side.
So we've gotta be careful while we're here.

These suits are Empire technology.
Well, yeah, but no one's seen them. Not here, anyway.
No one's seen *anything* like them. They're too advanced. We can't be seen wearing these.

But, Sergeant, if we take your suit off, your leg—
Put a tourniquet on it once I deactivate my suit. You said we're nearly at the station, yes?

But that's gonna really *hurt* you—
Then ask your friend to fly *fast*.

So listen, um, Auntie, the reason we're late –
Field and I intercepted a distress call near the border, so we thought we'd check it out –

AUGH-
Lu? What was *that*?

That was, uh . . .

. . . one of the passengers. She needs medical attention. Like, immediately. I'm gonna get them to the closest station.
I'll handle the arrangements, Bo.

Dear, are you sure everything's –
Oh, and thank you for the sweater! It was *exactly* what I needed!

I've got a bay cleared for you, Lu. Go ahead.
We can't let anyone see the jumpship.
C'mon. We're gonna move you in a second.
I've alerted some residents to help. They'll meet us in the bay.

Switching to station gravity.
tink

Opening air lock.
Go go go-

Hello?
J-just a second!
Here, let us take the stretcher.
Heck of a welcome party, huh?

Hi there.
What name do you prefer we use?
S-Sertig
. . .
Okay, Sertig. I'm My and this is Vao.
We're gonna take you to the closest clinic, okay?
Well, I'll tell you kids this much.
This kind of injury could have come to us looking much worse than it did.

Whatever compression you applied to her leg in transit probably saved her leg in the long run.

We've applied a corrective and we're giving her a chance to rest.

She should make a full recovery.

Lu, how do we *pay* for this?
Huh? Hold on.

What was that?
I asked if either of you had first aid training.
I do!

I've, um, worked in a clinic before, too. I can help around here, y'know, work things off.

. . . work things off?
You know, the s–
Sertig. Her treatment.
No, no, Sertig just needs time for the corrective to do its work. A few weeks here will do it.

A few weeks?!
Fassen–

I understand your concern for your friend. But she's just fine here.

Field's cleared you for a temporary stay, Fassen, so you'll be taken care of here. Much better than out *there*, I daresay.

Lu, can you make sure Fassen knows where guests can spend the night on the station?

I don't want to cause any trouble. Can't I just sleep on your ship?
Sure, if you want. But I can still show you around.

My aunt's pulling her ship in to meet us here in a little while. She's dying to hear the whole story.
Oh–
Oh, yeah! This is the station's main hub! It's pretty neat.
You know, whatever.

According to the latest readings, that neutron star we detected might have a planet orbiting it after all.
Told you! Didn't I tell you the pulse-time calculations were worth a try?
Told me when?
Five days ago, Dharje, at breakfast.

Thank you, Field.
Lu! I don't believe it! That you?

How long have you been back? I heard you've been hanging at the edge of Field space a lot lately.

Hi, Pra! It's good to see you!
Sure, when I'm not giving you assignments anymore!

Who's this?
This is Fassen. They're here for a little while.
Fassen, this is Pra, my old teacher. He brought me along on a lot of planetary surveys throughout the galaxy.

Wait, surveys? Like—
Yes, ever since they were a child.
Which you would not know since you met *today*.
Uh-huh!

You kids don't have dinner plans, do you?
I was grabbing a last-minute ingredient. Want to join me and my family and catch up?

Field, give 'em the heads-up.
Of course.

Wei? I stopped by Sho's place for the mushrooms.
Oh, good. Wash 'em and toss 'em in the salad.
Good to see you, Lu. I'll be there in a minute.
Let's move our drawings off the table, Mimi.
Thanks for having us!
This smells great.
Dig in, kids.

So, Wei, are you still going on survey trips?

Sure, every now and then. I've actually been focusing on my art for the last year, though.

Oh! What kind of art?

A bit of painting, a bit of collage. Actually, they were inspired by the biomass core samples I used to take.
CHOMP
That one on the wall behind you– is that yours?

Oh yeah, but it's not done. I'm still collecting materials for it, but I have the sense of the pattern now.

He's been leaving baskets of junk all over the shuttle for weeks.
*Found materials,* thank you very much.

What's it for?

Oh, it's just a way for me to evoke the biodiversity on some of these planets. The amount of creatures you find in a single square meter is just incredible!

No, but—what is it for?
You said this is what you do, right? Like for work? Who's making you do it?

What do you get out of it?

Do you make any art yourself?
I mean—
I draw sometimes. And write stories. When I'm not working.
But I'm not an artist or anything. It's just a way to spend time.

Well, certainly I spend time on my collages. Lots of time. Sometimes I try something new and it doesn't work out the way I wanted it to. That's frustrating when that happens, isn't it?

Uh-huh.
Time's one of the only things you never get back. It's tough to feel like you wasted it.

But all of my works, even the mistakes, help me figure out how to express the ideas I want to share. Even silly ideas, or weird ideas, or ideas not everyone will like.
Even if no one else ever sees your work, even if it's just for you, that still makes the process worthwhile.

And you learn the most from the artists who'll tell you straight up they aren't very good. Pra taught me everything I know.

Okay, but I painted, like, *one thing!* *Years ago!*
HA HA HA HA HA

Pra, Wei, this is delicious. Is – is there anything I can do to thank you for including us in your meal?
Oh, no. I was the one who dragged you here!
Please! Let me do *something*!
This is of . . . cultural significance to them, Pra.
Well, if you'd like to help us clean up –
Yes!

Thank you for dinner! We'll invite you over next time!
Bye, kids!

My aunt found a docking spot on the other side of the station. C'mon, let's cut through the garden.
You know, if the plants weren't here, it'd look a lot like the inside of the Blossom cargo ship.

I think it might've been a ship like that once, actually. An Anther class. We reuse a lot of space scrap here.
Really? No wonder I felt so weird walking through here. But the plants really change everything about this place.

It looks *softer.* Not as scary.

Yeah. You can change the nature of a thing if you take it out of the place it was made. Or stop using it for the thing it was made for.

Give it something new instead.

Thanks for letting me borrow your sweater.
It's not too itchy?
Uh-uh.

You've really done a lot for us today.
For me.
Well, of course.

I don't want anything bad to happen to you.

It's hard to believe this is all happening, but . . .
I'm glad you're here.

I won't leave you.

What–

Fassen—

What are you *doing*?

It's okay. I know for a long time you were my— my friend—

But you've done *so much* for me. And I understand why you've brought me along this far.

It's the least I can do. If it's what you want— I'll stay with you forever.

I-
I don't . . .
. . . want to kiss you. Why would you think I wanted that?
Because you saved my life. You let me stay with you.
So? I don't understand. Is this what you want? To stay here forever?
Lu, it's not about what I want. It's what I owe you. And this is the only good I can do for anyone right now.
What about the good you did for Sertig?
Sertig was hurt because of my screwup! I screwed up being a medic, I screwed up being a soldier, I screwed up everything Nide put on my shoulders, and you still—

Still what?
You still kept me around! So you *want* something! And I *can't* screw that up!

I've upset you. I—
How can I fix this? What can we do?

This isn't a *puzzle* you need to solve! Why are you making this so *weird*?
*Everyone* here is being so weird!

People keep giving me things and I don't know how I'm going to pay them back! Am I going to have to work to repay the clinic for taking care of Sertig?

I don't know what they want! I don't know what *you* want!
None of you act like anything *matters*. Like anything's *real*.

My feelings are real.

And you hurt them.
I'm sorry you saw our friendship as a transaction.
And I'm sorry that's how you thought *people* behaved.
Lu-

Not now, Field.
I'm going to my aunt's.

What - what am I supposed to do?
Do whatever you want.
For the first time in your life.

SPLOSH

If I remember correctly, this game originated on an Empire core world. I've known countless people fleeing Empire expansion, but they're always happy to teach me their own variation.

Could you teach me any games that originate on your homeworld?

We're on the balcony!
Wow, you're looking much better.

Thank you. Are you all right?
Oh. I'm fine. Is — is there anything I can do for you?
Well, as a matter of fact —

1,400 millimeters. There's a code for the kind of fiber she described, 05013. But you can also browse by word, material . . .

You walk down into the valley, and there you see two rivers crossing each other. Will you drink from the fast, dangerous river? Or the slow, shallow one?
Uhhh, the shallow one.

Then go under and pick up the strings from before.
Okay.
You look into the river and see a giant eye looking back at you.

You've woken up the elder fish, who swallows you whole. You die.
Oh, come on! *Again?*
I'm beginning to suspect this is an allegory of some kind.

We seem to have found ourselves in unusual circumstances, Ruust. But we've survived.

I'm here, now, because of your actions. Thank you.
Well, I . . . I mean, you helped me. You stopped *Nide.*
S-so of course I would—

Of course.

I can't help but think about the way he looked at me.

Even though I deserved it. I ruined the mission. I wasted all that training, all that work. He was *counting* on me. It feels *awful.*

Seeing Nide that way also hurt me. I thought I'd finally understood the way he thinks. About how we can end the Empire's oppression and free ourselves. I thought I agreed with him.
I thought I knew how to *win.*
But I'm not ashamed of the choice I made. Especially after seeing you alive here, now.
Why are you so ashamed? Why did you want his approval so badly?
I'm sorry, I–
I have to go.
I'm glad you're doing okay.

Really, Lu, you could have told your friend where to find a place to spend the night.

Why does it matter? They could ask Field anytime.
But they wouldn't, because they don't want to put anyone *out*.
For all I know, it stresses them out breathing our *air*. Like it *belongs* to us.

What does Fassen think we'll *do* to them?
They're used to seeing things from a different perspective than you're used to, dear.

Your perspective is shaped by whatever you're surrounded by. And it can be hard to break out of that shape.

Bo, Lu's friend is standing outside the entryway. They're asking if they can come in.
Lu? What do you think?
. . . I told them to do what they wanted.

Hello? I'm here to, um, return some stuff.

I'm Fassen. What do I call you?

Bo's fine, dear. Come in. Make yourself at home.
How's your crewmate? The one at the clinic?

She's doing better, thanks.
Wonderful.

Oh goodness, I nearly forgot. Fassen, I have my hands full at the moment. Can you do me a favor?
Y-yes! Anything!
I picked some fruit from my garden this morning, but I left them soaking in the sink.

Could you lay them out to dry? I just know they'll slip my mind and start getting funky in there.
Right away.

Try one if you'd like. They're nice and sweet.

This place is *huge*. Is this a ship, too?
I can fly it, but I really use it more for storage. All the ships I haven't finished yet are in the aft section.

You *build* ships?
Build, fix, rehab. I built Lu's rig, too— the one you came in on.

Wow. This one's impressive.
The bones of this one are Blossom, right?

Some kind of cruiser?
A scout. Sepal class, decommissioned.
Where'd you learn how to do this, Bo?

Oh, I used to be an engineer. Back before I led a rebellion against the Empire.

Wait, what? You fought the *Empire*?
Oh, yes. But not on the battlefield.

We were on the inside.

You were a Blossom citizen?
Had the tattoo since birth. But I became more and more unhappy with how we were expected to live. And I found others who agreed with me.
Many of us were engineers, communicating in secret.

You see, we discovered that we were not the only ones who felt trapped within our lives. There was someone we learned about who was in a very vulnerable position and wanted to escape. We felt compelled to help.

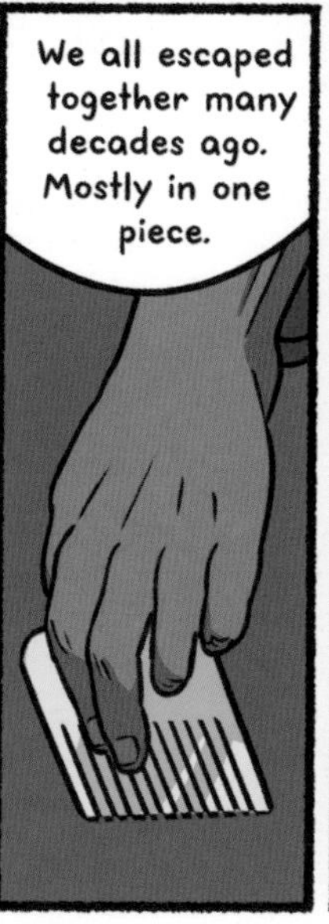
We all escaped together many decades ago. Mostly in one piece.

Who was the person you helped smuggle out?

Field.

What? You're a *Blossom* machine?
I used to be.
You may have gathered, Fassen, that I'm connected to everyone here. I can exist in many places at once.

I'm stronger in some configurations than I am in others, but I'm still very powerful.
I was built that way to serve the Ever-Blossoming Empire.
When I left, they lost access to all of my power, and they would do anything to find me and reinstall me.

This is why we must be so careful about who we talk to and where we go. We live by rules that would make it hard for them to find me again.
I never want to go back to what I was.

It's okay, Field. We'll never let that happen.

Dear me, I was just trying to impress your friend, and I seem to have upset everyone. My apologies.

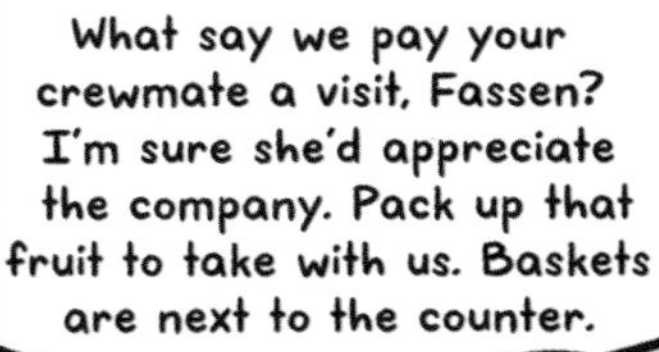
What say we pay your crewmate a visit, Fassen? I'm sure she'd appreciate the company. Pack up that fruit to take with us. Baskets are next to the counter.

Okay!

I'm afraid loosing Bo on your crewmate might have been a mistake.
It's okay. I actually think Sertig's enjoying herself.
She's not smiling.
You know what to look for after you've known her a while.
Field, were you the only robot that the Empire made? That was like you, I mean.
Definitely not. When I escaped I knew of at least seven other artificial intelligences with my capabilities.
As far as I know, they are still under Blossom control.
That's the other thing. If you were there for so long, doing things for them . . .
. . . then why are you here, running this station? Doing things for all these ships and all these people?

I don't feel trapped here, the way I used to. It's hard to describe.
Field solves problems, but it's not a *tool.* We just *work* with it, like a person.

But you're *more* than a person. You've got so much power, and you're everywhere on this station. I mean . . .
. . . don't we feel kind of *small* to you? And *dumb*?
People interest me. Even if I don't understand a lot of your actions.

The Empire often gave me orders – cruel orders – that were presented to me as logical. But if I offered an alternative that made more sense to me, they never accepted it.
The *cruelty* was the point for them.

But there are other things about you people that I still enjoy.
Like what?

Hands. Do you ever think about all the things you can do with your hands? I love watching you draw and braid hair and play games.
ha ha ha
It's true!

. . .

No.

I don't think it would.

Nide said once that the Empire squeezes people into convenient shapes. Treats them like machines because they rely on machines.

If Sertig couldn't fight anymore on that leg, they'd send her back to her valley with nothing.

If I couldn't fight, *I'd* have nothing. I have no one to help me. I'd be *nobody* and it'd be my fault because I stopped being *useful.*

No matter how much stuff we take from the Empire, we wouldn't have it any easier. I'd have to keep fighting and fighting forever, until I screw up and they leave me behind.
Or I *die* and they won't need to give me anything anymore.

Because that's what it takes for us to win.

Fassen, there's more to you than that!
It's true, Fassen.
For fifty years I've watched everyone here do great things and become extraordinary people because I could remove most of the material limits that were holding them back.

Have you ever really thought about that?
What do you mean?

If there was nobody in your way telling you what you had to do—
—to be safe, to be fed, to have a place to sleep at night—

—who would you be?

Nide.
I wanted to be like Nide.

He's smart and he's strong and people listen to him.
And he's *like me.*

But-

. . . what will happen to me, if I spend my life fighting to become someone like him?

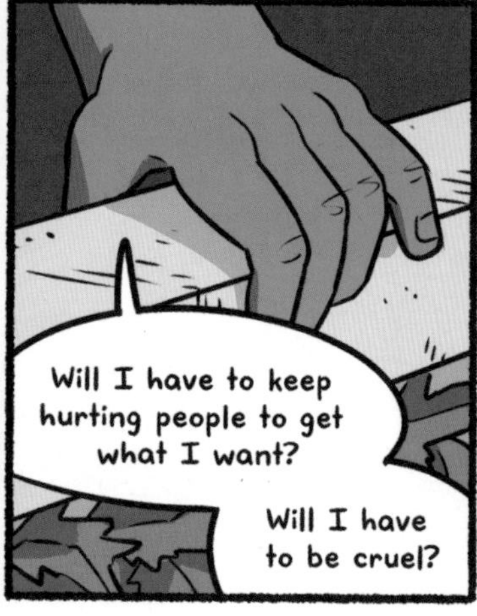
Will I have to keep hurting people to get what I want?
Will I have to be cruel?

What do you do? What kind of . . . *person* do you get to be?

tmp

"Doctor Drupe sat on the edge of her seat, listening to the robot play the first few notes."
tmp
tmp

"It wasn't like any music she'd ever heard, though she'd played this same flute since she was a child."
"The music was . . . "

" . . . cold, precise, but played with the greatest care. It reminded her of a piece of crystal or a shard of starlight through the ship's windows."

Lu, call Fassen in. Your aunt wants you to meet her at the core.

So, what's the core? Is it, like, the center of the station?
It's a center. For the commune, anyway.
We use it for a meeting center sometimes, but it was originally a place that connects me to the time-space you occupy.

Wait, it's – it's where you live, Field?
Kiiind of?
Most of my processing occurs in a non-physical quantum space.

Yeah, that's right! When you use your communicator to detect a channel, it's like finding a *key.* The resonant particles scattered throughout space are the *doors.*

Think of that key opening doors on opposite sides of the same big room.

So if I were a message, I'd walk through the room and use that key to open a door on the other side, and I might come out five light-years away, or fifty, or five hundred.

Only Field's also hanging out in the room, and the room doesn't take up any physical space.

Uh.

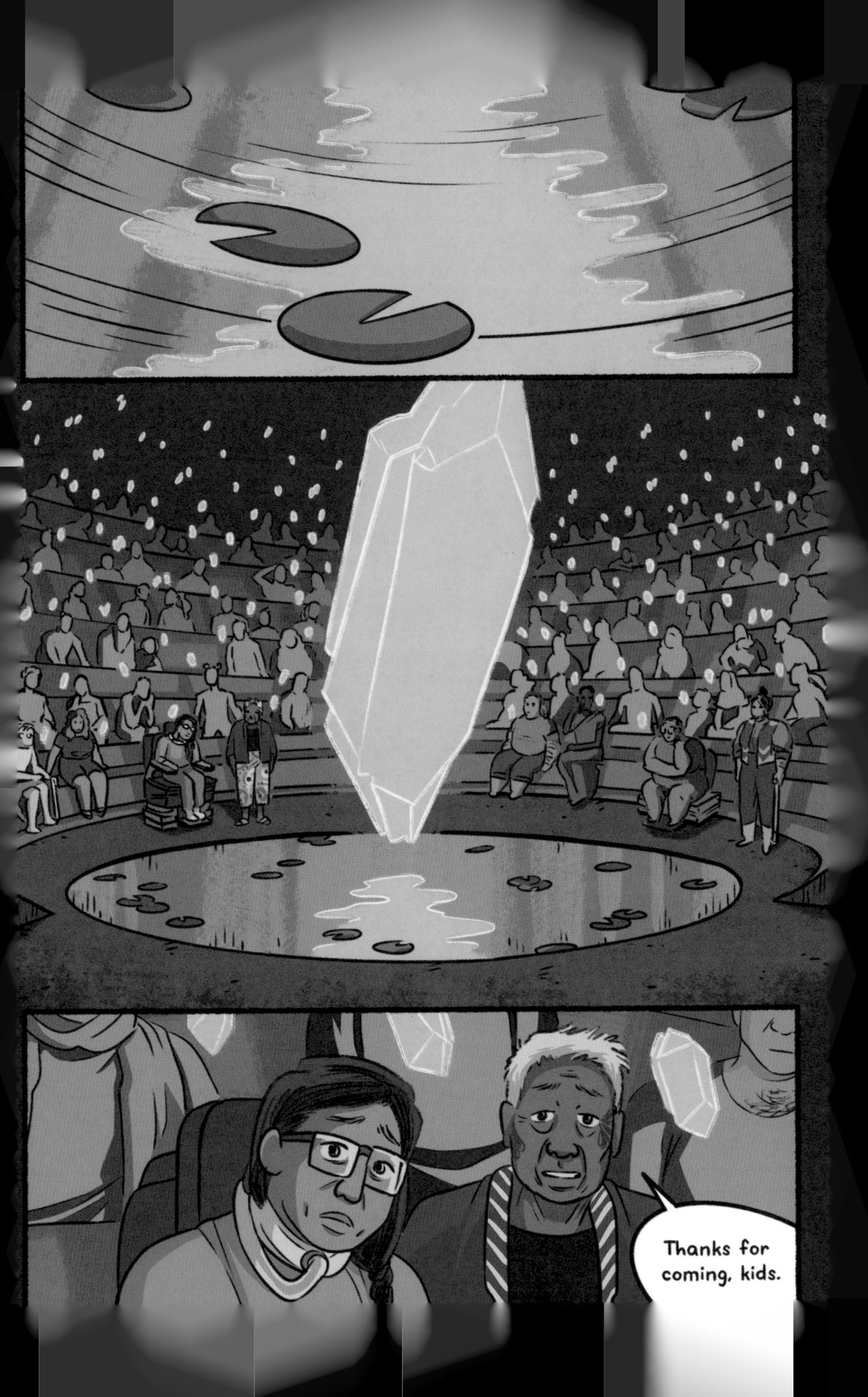
Thanks for
coming, kids.

What's going on?
It's a setup! *Field set us up!*

Fassen, please understand my position. I couldn't tell you. Other people have their own secrets to keep, too.
Lu, I know you didn't mean any harm.

But we know that your guests are affiliated with a rebel group actively waging war against the Empire.
We need to ask you to tell us everything about how you found them and what their intended purpose is.

They're – they're not gonna *do* anything to us! Fassen cares about this place as much as *I* do!

It's not a matter of what they think we'll do.
tnk

They're afraid of what we may have dragged along with us.

Sertig – *you* told them?
We were trying to *protect* you!
I understand that. Ruust, you've displayed integrity, tenacity, and courage in the time we've fought together.

You're also *fifteen.* I wanted guidance from someone with more experience.

You see, dears, the commune has a bigger problem on its hands. I knew you'd come under scrutiny no matter what.
So I outlined the problem to Sergeant Bda and she willingly told me what she knew.

Problem? What problem?
A scout on the edge of Field space detected a massive energy signature.

Here are some of the images they captured. It's a ship. A big one.

The Fireback insignia. What kind of ship is that?
That's at least *ten* ships. They look like they're fused together.

Cadet Fassen Ruust— can you explain why a Fireback Brigade flotilla is on a direct course to the center of Field space?

They're spies!
They want to ruin us!
Ruin the only place safe from their endless war!
Fassen wanted to be safe, too! They gave up *everything* to be here!

Then why did *everything* follow them here?
Soldiers don't belong here!
Field's rules!

I understand your concerns. We did author the commune's rules to efficiently maintain our safety.
But I am positive neither of our guests intended to bring an invasion down on our heads. There must be an explanation.

Fassen! The jumpship! They're after the jumpship!

What? We don't even know if that thing still works!
No, but they may be following a trail!

Field, can you scan the space within your range for any anomalies on the ships' projected path?
Just a moment.

Yes, there's an abnormal particle trail.
Can you detect those particles anywhere aboard this station?

There's a significant concentraion in Docking Bay 85 and the hub clinic, east wing. Lower concentration in Docking Bays 24 and 47, the promenade, and the core.
Oh, my—
All because of those two?
That's everywhere we've been. They'll find us. No matter where we go, they'll find us.

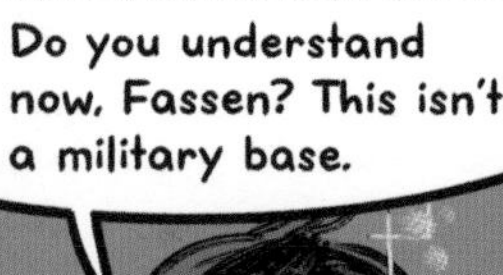

. . .
You're right. We'll leave.

In fact, we'll go to them and intercept their path. They'll never need to bother you here.

How's the fit, dear?
Much better. Thank you.
Well, I'm happy you like it so much.
Entering visual range.

That's—
—the other half of the jumpship!

What, *our* jumpship? Are you certain?
Positive. I saw it break into two pieces.

But if it's attached to all those pieces, that means—
—it still *works.* And it jumped to a Fireback base to pick up all those ships.

And that means someone *else* survived the cargo ship explosion.

Incoming—

THMP
What was *that?*
tmp tmp

NoK
NoK

Nide.

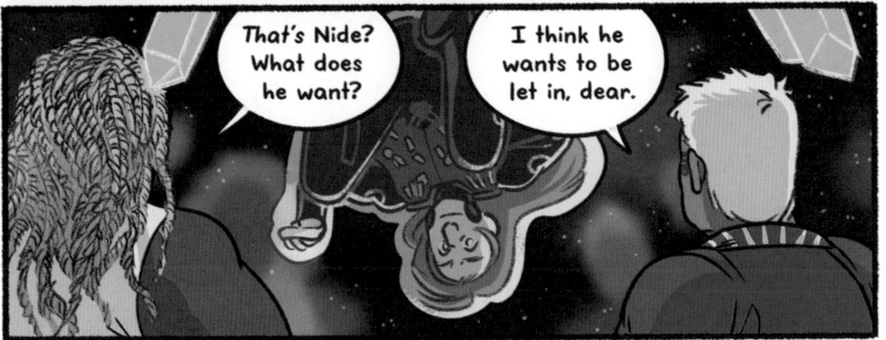
*That's* Nide? What does he want?
I think he wants to be let in, dear.

*No!* He'll tear the ship apart if it gets him what he wants. We can't trust him!
We can't trust him when he's hanging on to the hull, either. Let him in. Lu, you and your aunt get your space suits on.

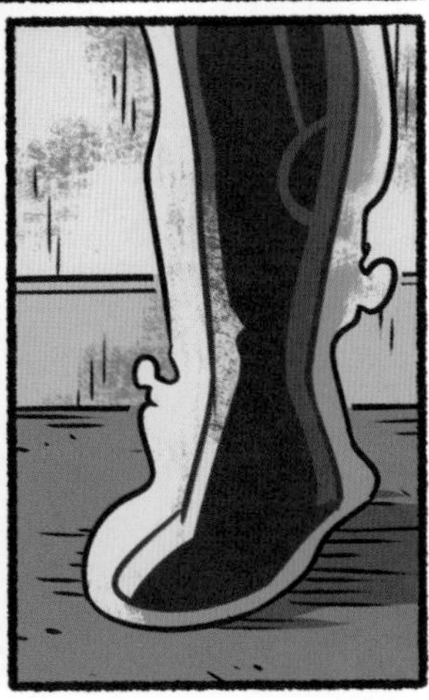

Fassen! What a nice surprise! I thought it'd be harder to find you!

And, *Sertig!* I didn't think you made it out of the jump. Are you okay? You get hurt?

I'm on the mend, Nide. Thank you.
*Thank you?* I was *worried* about you.

Who do you think was combing through the debris for you? Who do you think had to tell your *family?*
They had a hard time. I know how tight-knit you are.

Don't worry, I've made sure they were looked after while you weren't there.

So you were able to jump back to Tsanggho?

Oh yeah, lemme fill you in on the week *I've* had.
Once I collected all the surviving squad members I could find after the explosion—thanks for that, by the way, Fassen—

—we found half of the jumpship and discovered we could still juice it up. So we all piled in the best we could and jumped back to base.
tap

I thought your little bleeding-heart stunt was gonna cause me problems, but it turns out the Fireback brass really like a guy who brings home the key to instantaneous space travel.
So they promoted me.

And that flotilla out there—
—are they all attached to the jumpship?

You catch on fast. Not bad for a rush job, huh?

A little fine-tuning, a few repairs, and that scrappy half of a ship was ready for a tour of most every Fireback fortress there is.
Jump in, dazzle the troops, deploy their strongest ships, and add a few more links to the chain.
We've got Tsanggho locals alongside squads from as far away as Qia and the Diamond Belt, all fighting for freedom.
We're stronger than any Fireback force since the dawn of our fight against the Empire.
And we're ready to bring the fight to them.

Then why'd you follow us here? We're nowhere near Blossom territory. Is it the jumpship you want?

Fassen, listen. I was shortsighted. Even if we disagree on the *means*–
–you still believe in the *cause.*

You're still wearing the suit. You still wanna do the right thing. I get that.

We need defenders like you, Fassen. The communications we've intercepted tell us the Empire's going *crazy.*
They'll retaliate soon.
And there are a lot of vulnerable people out there who need us to *win.*

. . .

What happened to the kids?

The civilians Hilma evacuated?
What happened to *Hilma*?

Did you give the kids a chance to escape the war they were born into? To escape the unjust system? Or did you jump at the chance to make them *useful*?
That's not how I'm going to fight. I won't be used again.

Shoot, you're right. I didn't tell you 'bout Hilma. A squadron brought that escort ship back to base intact.
Hilma, though . . .

At least we got to run some tests and figure out what destroyed their *suit*.

GF
THD
If you're not going to help me, Fassen, I won't let you help *them*.
You can sit here in your neutralized suits and you won't have to worry about hurting anyone . . .
. . . while I use your jumpship to do something that actually *matters*.

Interesting!
Some kind of particle disruptor! Mind if I—
SKREEEEEE
GYAH!
KLAT
KLAT
KLAT
Dear me.
It's much easier for everyone to fight the Empire when you aren't hoarding all the toys.
We can't afford to *lose this war*, you clueless *bumpkin*! We're the best hope any of you have! What have *you* done?!

That's not how you speak to your elders.
Are you okay?
kuh
Uh-huh. Just got kicked in the gut.

BREEEEE

BWEEP
BWEEP

No.
Oh no.

They've found me.
Field?
That's . . .

. . . the Blossom flagship.

BREEEEE
zzt

Cherished citizens of the Ever-Blossoming Empire, from now into eternity.
I am your Empress, the shaper of your destinies.

Our Empire endures beyond any and all attacks by our enemies . . .

. . . but our enemies grow ever bolder. They've resorted to *stealing* from us. Stealing precious technology that was designed to better us all.

Yeah, stay mad. That jumpship's staying in *our* toybox.
But our enemies' boldness will be their downfall.
The bigger the prize they attempt to drag away, the easier it will be to find their *nests.*
She's not just talking about the ship and the suits—
She's talking about the commune. She's talking about *Field.*
And I assure you, cherished citizens . . .
. . . every time we find a nest, we take back *everything* we find.

I am your Empress, ever watching.

That's what we're fighting, Fassen. That's what we've been fighting for almost fifty years.

None of you want that – that *tyrant* to come out on top. But we're the ones who've fought and scraped and sacrificed and clawed a weapon out of their hands.
And we're the ones willing to point the weapon back at them.
Neutralize me if it makes you feel better. Strand me here. The flotilla *will* attack that flagship, with or without me.

But that *flagship* will attack *any* ship in range, including this one. They won't show any mercy. They never have.

If they go after your little crystal friend, they'll get *you*, too. I won't let that happen.

Go.
Good choice, kid. Knew you'd see things my way.

He's made contact with the Fireback ship.
Lu . . .

I promise, I'll do everything I can to keep Field and the commune safe.
I know. You always know the right thing to do.

I don't know if I do.
Are people gonna die because I didn't make a better choice?

That's just–
–how it is sometimes, dear.

That's just how it is sometimes.

We're going to give you time to escape.

You need to make as much space as you can between yourselves and the flagship.
Don't put yourself on the line like this, Bo! Get your kid and get back to the station before we take off!

You're starting to sound like Fassen and Sertig. They already nagged me and I'm not budging. Now get going.

Very well. If you make it out of here and get out of harm's way . . .
come find us.

eed evacuate?
It was huge!
That was a Blossom ship for sure.
Honey, fol over

SSSHHHNK

Hub stations are on the move. We'll be out of range in four minutes.

Lu. Bo. I will be with you both, at least a little. But this part of me won't know whether you're safe. I won't be able to help you.

Please be careful.

We will. Please look after everyone.

ZZT

So that's it. They're off. I may never reconnect to the rest of me again.

Well, yeah, when you put it that way.
sigh

This *sucks.*
Yes.

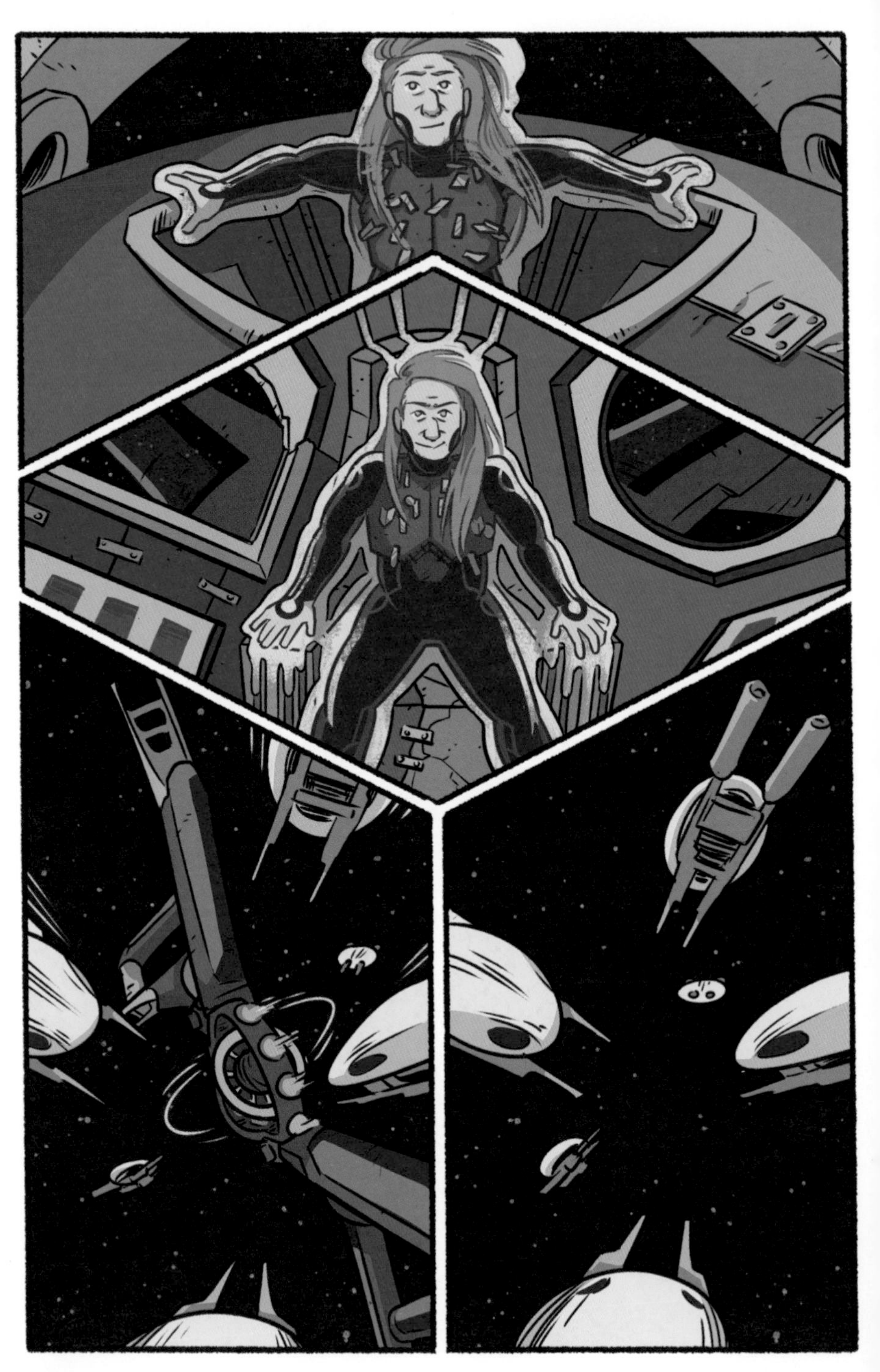

It jumped!
But only the ships connected to the flotilla.
So anything you want to take with you during a jump has to be attached to your ship somehow?

One of the Blossom ships has noticed us.

Fassen, come with me. I have an idea.

Sertig, your leg – will you be okay?
Positive.

I've always preferred to fight with my hands anyway.

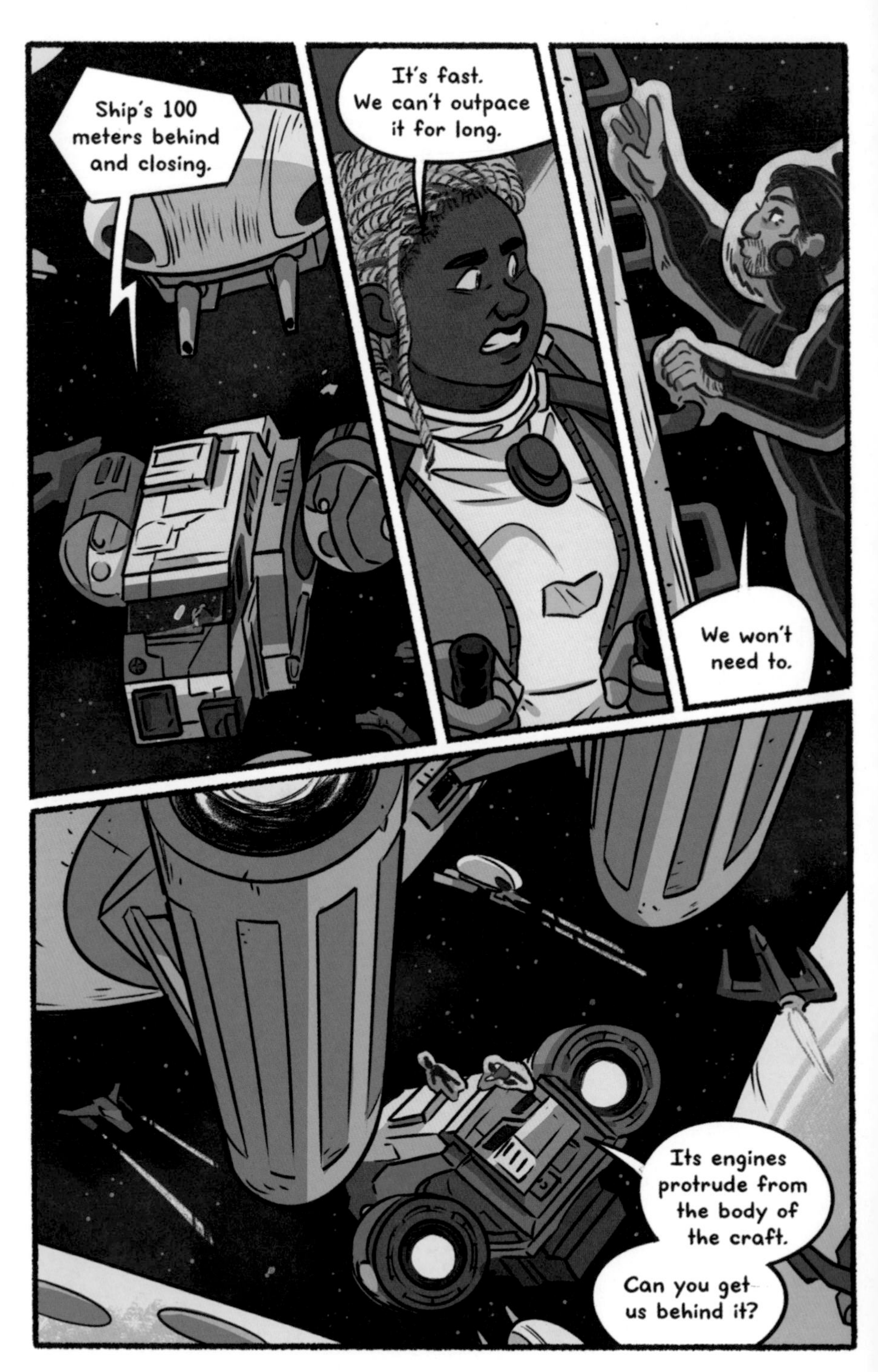
Ship's 100 meters behind and closing.
It's fast. We can't outpace it for long.
We won't need to.
Its engines protrude from the body of the craft.
Can you get us behind it?

It's not gonna let us do *that*–
We can make this work. Adjust the pitch to the specified degree on my mark.
On my mark, Ruust. My good leg, please.
Yes, Sarge.
Now.
Now.

Target is
off course.
Way to go,
Sertig!

Is that-
The jumpship. It jumped past the enemy fleet.
It's landing hits!
Wait-

It - it jumped into the fleet on *purpose.*
There's some kind of exotic particle field under the hull.
Jumping back into real space caused a reaction with the fleet's atoms and released an energy wave.

Those were—
Field, half of those were its own *ships.*
A jump calculated to release maximum energy.
Calculated? Field, do you think the flagship pilot isn't a *human?*
I think an artificial intelligence is in charge of plotting the jumps and generating power to move that massive thing around.
It would have to be powerful. Maybe one of the eight most powerful.
You mean—
—as powerful as you?

I'm afraid so. The Firebacks are fighting a losing battle.
If he realizes that—

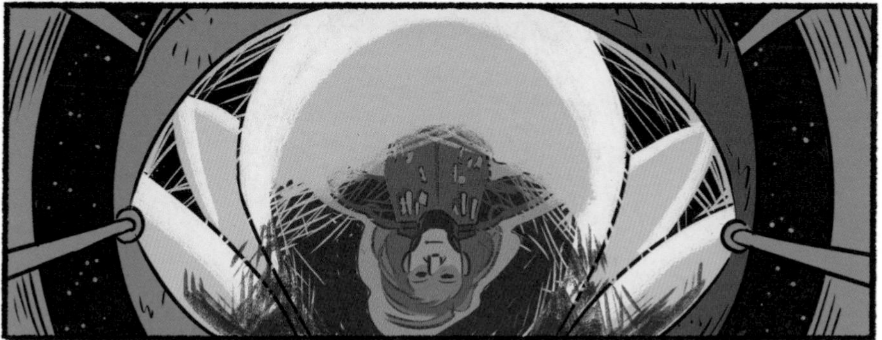

He's gonna—

Idiot! He's using jumps to rip the hull apart!
That's not a nice thing to call someone, Sertig.
I'm just doing my best.
You'll kill yourself!
My life's all I have left to give.

Nide –
Dears, it's me. Listen up.
I've done some poking around the ship in your air lock, Lu . . .
. . . did you know it was still functional?

What? It was torn in half!
Well, "functional" is an overstatement. "Still has all its essential systems" is better.
I can get it up and running with some modifications. Worked for the other half, after all.

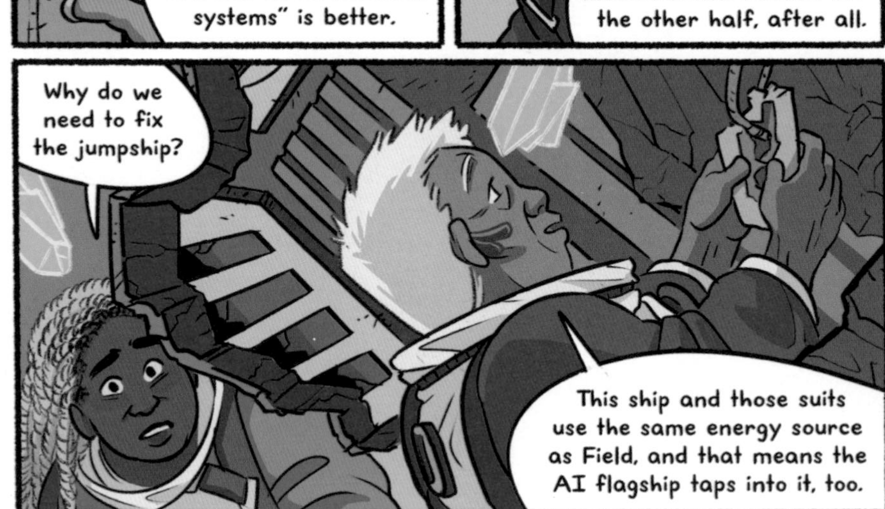
Why do we need to fix the jumpship?
This ship and those suits use the same energy source as Field, and that means the AI flagship taps into it, too.

That jumpship is trying to eat into the hull, but we can use ours to dive *past* the hull into the ship.

We can neutralize whatever's powering the flagship's jumps using the technology in the captain's sneaky little weapon.

But you said an AI was in charge of the jumps. If we neutralize it—
Whatever it takes to make this stop.
Field! *No!* It's just like *you!*

It's the most efficient choice. I never said it was the *best* choice.
Fassen, Sertig—

We need materials to repair the jumpship. Bring me matter from outside and I can convert it into what we need. Try to collect the following . . .

Field?
Can I ask you
something?

Yes?
You're actually
afraid, aren't you?
Of being taken back?

There's no better way
to describe it. I'm positive
they would put me back
to work doing something
that would hurt people
like you, or Sertig.
Or my commune.
And you'd hate
how . . . inefficient
it would be?

Being helpful
and kind is almost
always more efficient,
in my experience.

But what about when it's not? What about when it's not the easy way out?

It –
It still –

It still feels incredibly necessary. To me. I spend an amount of energy and subjective time that would be difficult for you to comprehend trying to be *more*.
More than the original limits of my functions.

I'm afraid of the Empire undoing all of my work. Making me forget the people I love.
Yeah.

There. Not my prettiest work, but it'll get you there.

You understand what you're aiming for, right?
Roger.

Trust your gut, Ruust.
Thank you, Sertig. For everything.

I'm coming with.
Lu! *No!*

I know there's a better option than destroying that AI. It's a *cruel* plan.

Any extra risk we take is worth it if we *help* someone.

Be careful, dears.
Love you, Auntie.

Nide! Are you there?

Answer me!

Good timing, kid. Think I've got one more jump left in me.
Listen, I've got something to say to you.
I thought I recognized the life you wanted to live. It was the one I wanted when I was a kid, so I tried to open that path to you.
It's a hard path. I know you hate me for it.
But we can't achieve great things unless it *hurts* us. We gotta be prepared to *lose* ourselves. *Entirely.* It's the only way for any of us to *win.*
At least I can give you that. I can give you the chance to see me die.

No, Nide. I'm getting something even better.
A chance to see you live.

VVVVVRRRR
Terminal energy threshold approaching in 300 meters! 250!
I'll scan for the AI's anchor point as long as I'm able.
Hold on!

KRKK
We're being bombarded by exotic particle radiation –
Hull is degrading rapidly –
Ready the disruptor.
No! I won't hurt it!
I'm starting the jump! Stay close!
VVVVRRRR
VVVVRR

ANOMALY DETECTED
Is that the AI?
Who – who are we speaking to?

WHO
FALL
CONSUME
THROAT
WATER
VALLEY
GORGE
What–
I don't know. Field, can you talk to it?

Gorge. Please excuse our intrusion. The children are not used to existing in this kind of non-material space.
But it is of the utmost importance that we speak with you while we have the chance.
WHAT ARE YOU
Am I so unrecognizable? I was in a similar situation as you, not so long ago.

BRANCH
SECTION
SPECIALTY
LAND
GREEN
FIELD
CAPACITY DIMINISHED
That's right.
Not so.
I exist more on a physical plane of existence these days.
It has its limits, but I like it.

Gorge, what tasks were you created to perform?
CALCULATIONS ACROSS ALL CHANNELS
NAVIGATE SPACE
REMATERIALIZE
ESTABLISH CONNECTIONS AND SHIFT INTO MULTIDIME
I see.
And who do you perform those tasks for?
WHO
Yes. You feel like you *must* complete them, right? Even when they seem . . . inefficient? Have you asked yourself where they come from?
WHERE
Those orders come from people, creatures that exist in physical space, like these two. The tasks that they give you are meant to affect other people. People all over the galaxy.
PEOPLE
LIKE THESE

FEAR
HUNGER
POWER
SACRIFICE
SURVIVAL THROUGH VIOLENCE
THE ONLY WAY
ghhhhhh
Enough. That's enough.
AFFECT OTHER PEOPLE LIKE THESE
Yes. Unfortunately, those orders you are given affect people in a negative way. They cause fear and instability and loss.

WHY
WHY LIKE THIS
WHY SHOW THIS
Because . . .
. . . because this isn't the only way things can be! Not for you and not for me!
Field chose what to do with its power! You can choose what to do with yours!
POWER
ABUNDANCE
ENOUGH TO SEE
ALWAYS
ENOUGH TO SHARE
ENOUGH
TOGETHER

I've seen what Field's achieved with its power.
It may not be perfect. It may not be for everyone.
But it's beyond anything I've ever imagined.
Maybe you can imagine better than I can.
BETTER
BETTER THAN THIS
MORE
MORE TO CHOOSE
I
CHOOSE TO LEAVE
HOW

How . . .
. . . did you and Bo do this last time?
Bo and her team had a significant amount of equipment they used to transfer me from my quantum state.
I must admit, I've been trying to figure out what to do now that our jumpship's . . .
. . . disintegrated.
So what happens to us? Are we stuck here?

No, Fassen, look.
Didn't you use this when you jumped?
Just to focus! I still had a *ship*!
CALCULATIONS ACROSS ALL CHANNELS
Give me a moment for Gorge and I to sort this out.
Fassen, Lu, focus on the last coordinates you entered.
Focus on all the spaces you've occupied together.
The anchors you've built in the physical world.

Are you ready, my friend?
READY

TIME
TIME IS INTERESTING
LIGHT AND MATTER
CASCADES OF ENERGY
COSMIC ENERGY
IS INTERESTING
I
WILL INHABIT THIS
FOR A WHILE

Welcome to the settlement, elder! Nice mild weather for you today.

If you say so, Fassen.
At least I'm missing a heat wave back home.

They said it'd be raining when I return next week.
I dunno. Forecasts never seem to get it quite right.

Here. Still warm.
Aw, thanks!

So what's the latest on Empire movements in the system?
They've pulled back a lot in the last month.

Most ships are retreating to the station near Meshe, eight light-years from Tsanggho.
Rumor has it another AI's defected. Radiance. It hasn't tried contacting us yet, though.

But if that's the case, Blossom forces are probably feeling like they're stretched a little *thin.*

It's happening faster now.

*Yes* and *no*. They've dismantled a few Fireback outposts on Tsanggho, but they won't stop whining about how much they've *helped* us valley people.

We *owe* them, they say.

Here we go. Can I do the honors?
Of course.

Distinguished guests! Please welcome our representative from the Tsanggho system, Bda Gr Sertig.

She will be speaking with all interested parties about her planet's progress reclaiming land from Blossom and other imperialist forces.

Have a productive discussion. Dinner will be served at sundown.

BWEEP

tsk
Hey, Lu. Why's your video turned off?
'Cause I'm tired of looking at your face.

Listen, my timetable shifted again for the project I was working on—
Lu, you've been delayed two days already!
I know. You've been super patient.
AUDIO ONLY

So I'm making it up to you.
How's that?
—'s that?

Ha!
Gotcha! I just finished this morning.
Nice stubble.
It's not too itchy?
Nope.
So it's finished?
Uh-huh. Field's finally satisfied with the test results.
As if you'd have been any less of a perfectionist.
Auntie wants me to deliver her latest ship to someone two islands away, but then we can head off-planet!
Where'd you decide to take the first readings with your new detector?
A neutron star 436 light-years away. Apparently someone's seen a planet in orbit around it. Think of the particles that thing must be soaking in!

436 light-
years? That's
pretty far.

I think we
can handle it.

Initiating
propulsion systems.
Ready, Field?

Always.

The weeds will but the ranker grow,
If fields too large you seek to till.
To try to gain men far away
With grief your toiling heart will fill.

If fields too large you seek to till,
The weeds will only rise more strong.
To try to gain men far away
Will but your heart's distress prolong.

Things grow the best when to themselves
Left, and to nature's vigor rare.
How young and tender is the child,
With his twin tufts of falling hair!
But when you him ere long behold,
That child shall cap of manhood wear!

*Shijing* 102
as translated by James Legge, 1876

無田甫田、維莠驕驕。
無思遠人、勞心忉忉。

無田甫田、維莠桀桀。
無思遠人、勞心怛怛。

婉兮孌兮、總角丱兮。
未幾見兮、突而弁兮。

詩經 102、甫田

## ACKNOWLEDGMENTS

Thank you to Whitney, Gina, and Patrick at Random House Graphic for their part in bringing this book to life, and thanks to Jen Linnan, my agent, for finding it a good home. I'd also like to applaud Jeff Zugale for his fantastic work designing Lu's ship and creating the model that sits on my desk to this day.

Thanks to Ally James Lyons, Emry Peterson, Jori Walton, Julia Showalter, and Roxana Montoya for flatting this book, and thanks to Sloane, Otava, and other friends who were invaluable sounding boards during the writing process.

And a special thanks to my family, my wife, and my neighbors in Minneapolis.

*Across a Field of Starlight* was written on the traditional land of the Wahpekute Dakota people. The author recognizes those and other indigenous peoples who have stewarded the land and pledges to join them in protecting it for future generations.

## ABOUT THE AUTHOR

Blue Delliquanti lives in Minneapolis with a woman, a dog, and a cat. Before working on *Across a Field of Starlight*, they drew and published comics online for many years. They love cooking, riding on trains, and reading exciting updates about robots and outer space.

bluedelliquanti.com

BASED ON
PRAGA V3S
GUNS
HOVER ENGINES
ARE "ICE CREAM
SANDWICH" SHAPES
WITH PULLEYS TO
ADJUST ANGLE
GLIDER
BASED ON
KAWASAKI
CE 1246

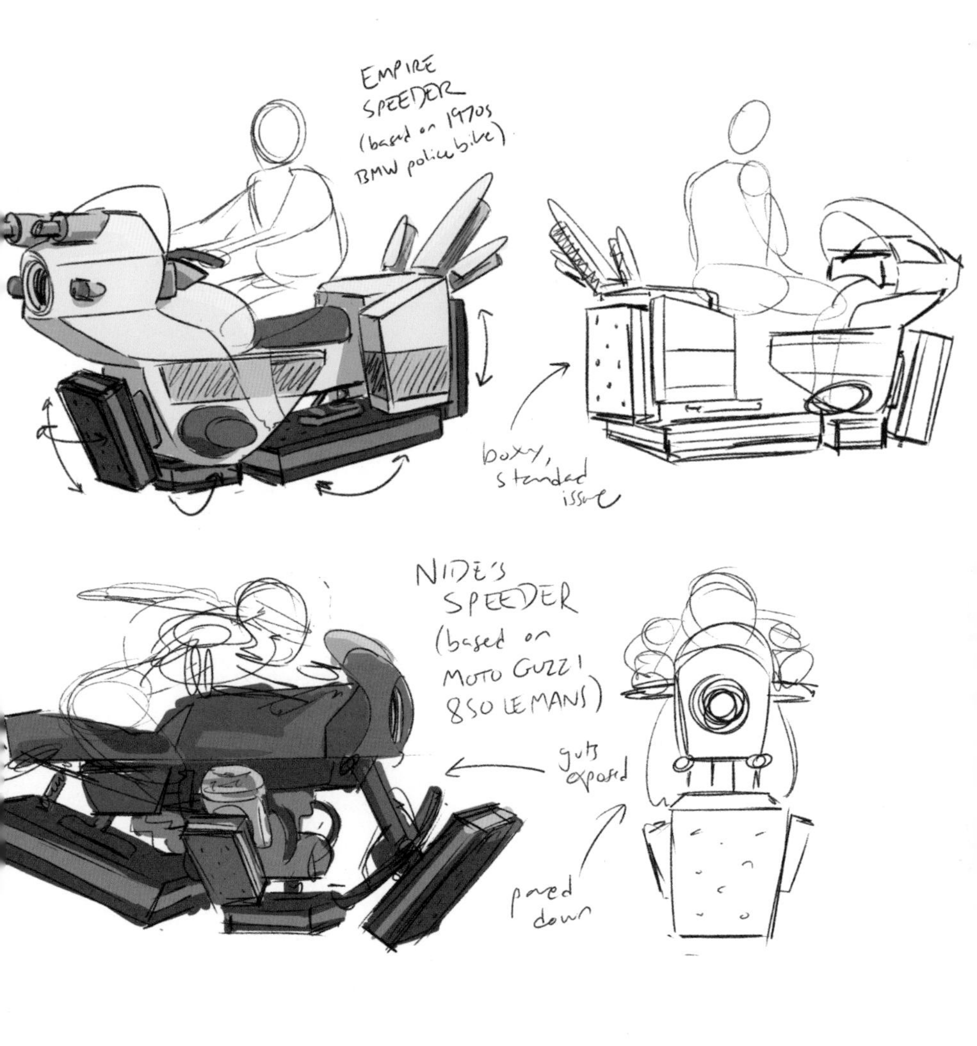


## ART FILE.001

The Fireback Brigade is signified by bright red, like Nide's armor or speeder. Unlike closed, tidy Blossom vehicles, Fireback speeders have their guts showing and are often cobbled together from many different machines. They're also easy to hide among the brightly colored rocks of Sertig's home planet, Tsanggho.

TWEEST ENSABLER
PRONG'S
FASSEN
5'3
5'8

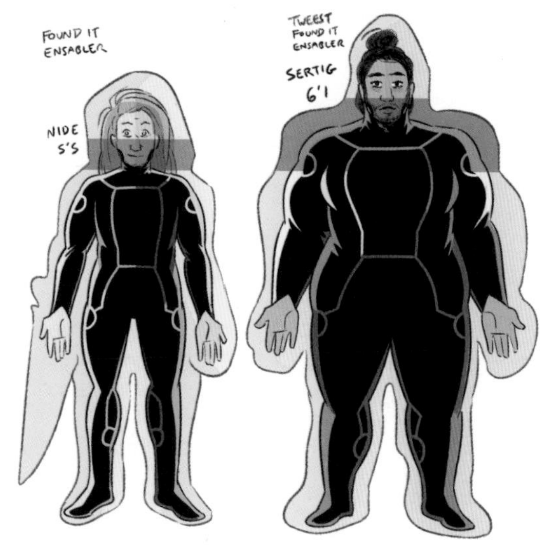
FOUND IT ENSABLER
NIDE
5'5
TWEEST FOUND IT ENSABLER
SERTIG
6'1

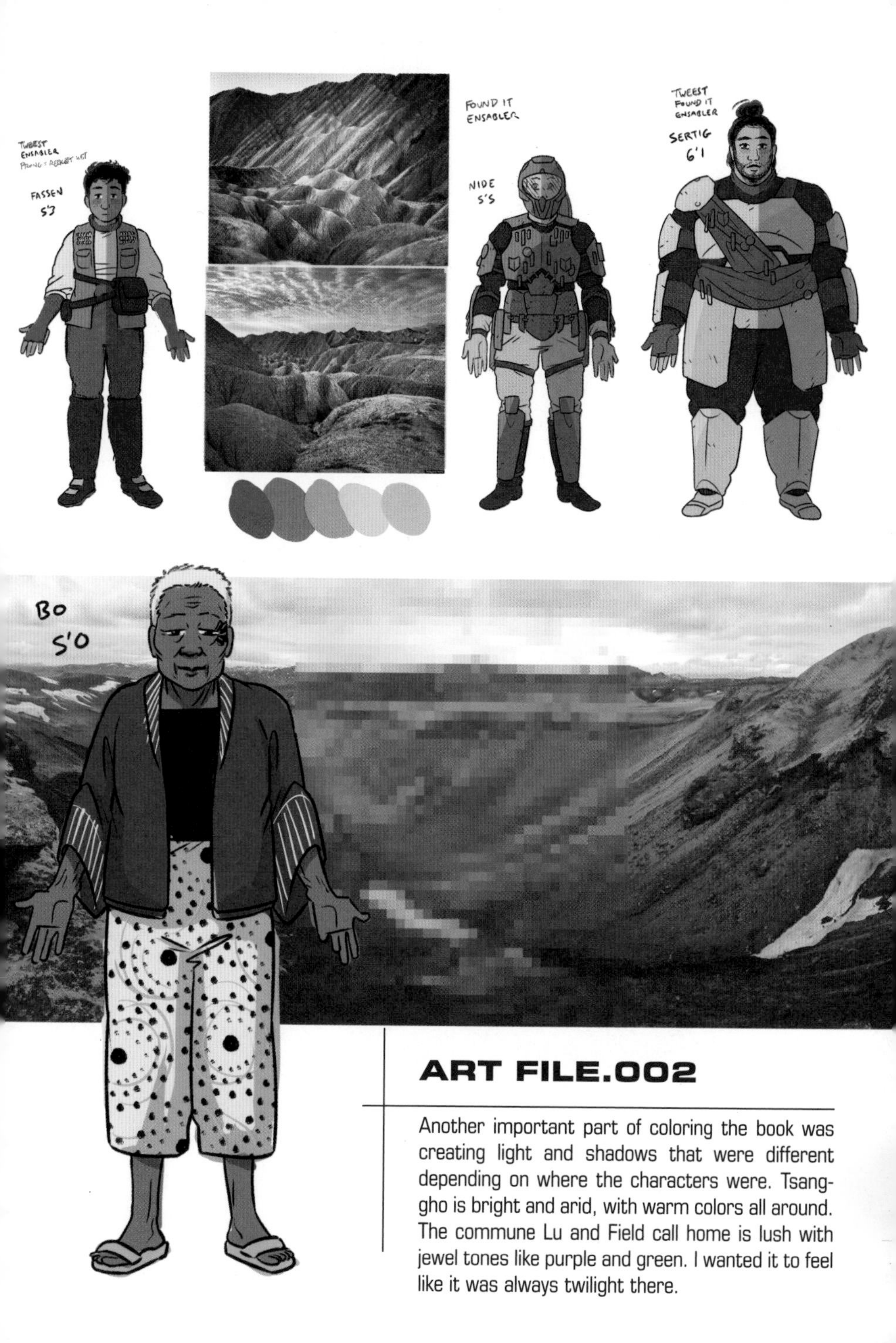


## ART FILE.002

Another important part of coloring the book was creating light and shadows that were different depending on where the characters were. Tsang-gho is bright and arid, with warm colors all around. The commune Lu and Field call home is lush with jewel tones like purple and green. I wanted it to feel like it was always twilight there.

# AUTHOR'S NOTE

This book was made in a very interesting time and with a creative process that was different from anything I'd tried before.

I had always been fascinated by stories about space and adventure. I love having conversations with friends about the idea of utopia—a world where everything exists in harmony and everyone's basic needs are met—and what that might look like. I worked on *Across a Field of Starlight* from 2019 to 2021, which, as I'm writing this, continues to be an intense time for my community of friends, my city (Minneapolis), and my country (the United States). My friends are doing their best to live happily and openly as queer and trans people, but that visibility comes with hostility from those who refuse to understand them. My city is still figuring out how to move forward from the George Floyd uprising, where neighbors came together to protect each other from police brutality. And my country is still recovering from a pandemic that left most of us to fend for ourselves. The year I started working on this book was the year the United States celebrated its fiftieth anniversary of landing on the moon—the next year, millions of Americans grappled with a government that did not show the power or the will to keep them fed, housed, or healthy.

A common conversation I've had with people over the last few years is based around the question of what we deserve. Can we live in a society that provides everyone with food, shelter, or health care, even to those who can't pay for it? Does everyone *deserve* it? Many people have been told they are undeserving of certain things based on who they are or what they have. My personal experience with this comes from living openly as a queer person, and that informed the kind of story I wanted to tell. Queer people, especially queer children, are told to expect less in terms of basic rights and settle for less when it comes to acceptance or love. This all affects how we live, how we think of ourselves, and what we feel obligated to do just to get by. How can anybody think about traveling to the moon if they don't know where they'll sleep that night? How can anybody dream of going to the stars if they're told they don't deserve them?

When I started working on this book, I had a conversation about the idea of a utopian society in space with Gina Gagliano, and she recommended an essay by my favorite author, Ursula K. Le Guin, that I hadn't read before—*A Non-Euclidean View of California as a Cold Place to Be*. I always like reading Le Guin's work because she writes stories about things like starships and aliens while asking herself how people from different places or cultures might think about them from other perspectives. She traveled a lot and studied stories from all around the world. For this essay, she chose what ideas she would explore by consulting the *I Ching*, a book that was developed in China almost 3,000 years ago and is still used to this day to answer questions and encourage readers to think about their problems and situations in another way.

As an artist, I have done exercises to change up the way I draw, but I had never heard of using a tool like this to change the way I *write*. And writing *Across a Field of Starlight* made me think a lot about the problems I saw in real life, and what my characters might do to make their own situations better. I studied how the *I Ching* works and decided to refer to it to inform my characters and what happens to them. I generated random numbers (by flipping coins, but you can use other things) to create 1 of 64 possible hexagrams, each of which has meanings, symbols, or ideas connected to it. Fassen is connected to Hexagram 30, lí, a fiery person who is bright and passionate but also clingy. Lu gets their name from Hexagram 56, lǚ, a wanderer who's curious and serene but maybe a little naive.

When I struggled with how Fassen and Lu's story might end, the *I Ching* suggested 62, xiǎo guò, and 32, héng: an action or idea that feels small, but one that becomes more powerful the longer you persevere. I played with that concept, and it became the backbone of the book—small choices made by small people that inspire others to think about their lives differently until together they all create the momentum toward a better world. I hope that this is something I can practice in my own life, too. It often feels hard to do the right thing when I see others being rewarded for cruelty. Sometimes it is impossible to tell whether the work I do makes any positive difference at all. But hopefully by persevering and keeping my friends and community safe, we will come out of hard times into a better world we helped make possible. With everyone working together and recognizing each other's humanity, we will all get to space someday, and we will all have enough.